Wealth and beggary, virtue and vice, repletion and the direst hunger, all treading on each other and crowding together

1 3 5 7 9 10 8 6 4 2

Vintage
20 Vauxhall Bridge Road,
London SW1V 2SA

Vintage Classics is part of the Penguin Random House group of companies whose addresses can be found at global.penguinrandomhouse.com

Penguin Random House UK

This edition published by Vintage in 2020

penguin.co.uk/vintage

A CIP catalogue record for this book is available from the British Library

ISBN 9781784876081

Typeset in 10.5/14.5 pt FreightText Pro
by Jouve (UK), Milton Keynes
Printed and bound in Great Britain by Clays Ltd, Elcograf S.p.A.

London

CHARLES DICKENS

VINTAGE MINIS

Contents

A TOUR OF DICKENS'S LONDON

Arriving, with Oliver Twist

'GOING TO LONDON?' said the strange boy, when Oliver had at length concluded.

'Yes.'

'Got any lodgings?'

'No.'

'Money?'

'No.'

The strange boy whistled; and put his arms into his pockets, as far as the big coat-sleeves would let them go.

'Do you live in London?' inquired Oliver.

'Yes. I do, when I'm at home,' replied the boy. 'I suppose you want some place to sleep in to-night, don't you?'

'I do, indeed,' answered Oliver. 'I have not slept under a roof since I left the country.'

'Don't fret your eyelids on that score,' said the young gentleman. 'I've got to be in London to-night;

and I know a 'spectable old gentleman as lives there, wot'll give you lodgings for nothink, and never ask for the change – that is, if any genelman he knows interduces you. And don't he know me? Oh, no! Not in the least! By no means. Certainly not!'

The young gentleman smiled, as if to intimate that the latter fragments of discourse were playfully ironical; and finished the beer as he did so.

This unexpected offer of shelter was too tempting to be resisted; especially as it was immediately followed up, by the assurance that the old gentleman referred to, would doubtless provide Oliver with a comfortable place, without loss of time. This led to a more friendly and confidential dialogue; from which Oliver discovered that his friend's name was Jack Dawkins, and that he was a peculiar pet and protege of the elderly gentleman before mentioned.

Mr Dawkins' appearance did not say a vast deal in favour of the comforts which his patron's interest obtained for those whom he took under his protection; but, as he had a rather flighty and dissolute mode of conversing, and furthermore avowed that among his intimate friends he was better known by the sobriquet of 'The Artful Dodger,' Oliver concluded that, being of a dissipated and careless turn, the moral precepts of his benefactor had hitherto been thrown away upon him. Under this impression, he secretly resolved to cultivate the good opinion of the old gentleman as quickly as possible; and, if he found the Dodger incorrigible, as he more than half suspected he should, to decline the honour of his farther acquaintance.

As John Dawkins objected to their entering London before nightfall, it was nearly eleven o'clock when they reached the turnpike at Islington. They crossed from the Angel into St John's Road; struck down the small street which terminates at Sadler's Wells Theatre; through Exmouth Street and Coppice Row; down the little court by the side of the workhouse; across the classic ground which once bore the name of Hockley-in-the-Hole; thence into Little Saffron Hill; and so into Saffron Hill the Great: along which the Dodger scudded at a rapid pace, directing Oliver to follow close at his heels.

Although Oliver had enough to occupy his attention in keeping sight of his leader, he could not help bestowing a few hasty glances on either side of the way, as he passed along. A dirtier or more wretched place he had never seen. The street was very narrow and muddy, and the air was impregnated with filthy odours.

There were a good many small shops; but the only stock in trade appeared to be heaps of children, who, even at that time of night, were crawling in and out at the doors, or screaming from the inside. The sole places that seemed to prosper amid the general blight of the place, were the public-houses; and in them, the lowest orders of Irish were wrangling with might and main. Covered ways and yards, which here and there diverged from the main street, disclosed little knots of houses, where drunken men and women were positively wallowing in filth; and from several of the door-ways, great ill-looking fellows were cautiously emerging, bound, to all appearance, on no very well-disposed or harmless errands.

Oliver was just considering whether he hadn't better run away, when they reached the bottom of the hill. His conductor, catching him by the arm, pushed open the door of a house near Field Lane; and drawing him into the passage, closed it behind them.

From *Oliver Twist*

From Saffron Hill, head south to Bleeding Heart Yard

In London itself, though in the old rustic road towards a suburb of note where in the days of William Shakespeare, author and stage-player, there were Royal hunting-seats – howbeit no sport is left there now but for hunters of men – Bleeding Heart Yard was to be found; a place much changed in feature and in fortune, yet with some relish of ancient greatness about it. Two or three mighty stacks of chimneys, and a few large dark rooms which had escaped being walled and subdivided out of the recognition of their old proportions, gave the Yard a character. It was inhabited by poor people, who set up their rest among its faded glories, as Arabs of the desert pitch their tents among the fallen stones of the Pyramids; but there was a family sentimental feeling prevalent in the Yard, that it had a character.

As if the aspiring city had become puffed up in the very ground on which it stood, the ground had so risen about Bleeding Heart Yard that you got into it down a flight of steps which formed no part of the original approach, and got out of it by a low gateway into a maze of shabby streets, which went about and about, tortuously ascending to the level again. At this end of the Yard and over the gateway, was the factory of Daniel Doyce, often heavily beating like a bleeding heart of iron, with the clink of metal upon metal.

The opinion of the Yard was divided respecting the derivation of its name. The more practical of its inmates abided by the tradition of a murder; the gentler and more imaginative inhabitants, including the whole of the tender sex, were loyal to the legend of a young lady of former times closely imprisoned in her chamber by a cruel father for remaining true to her own true love, and refusing to marry the suitor he chose for her. The legend related how that the young lady used to be seen up at her window behind the bars, murmuring a love-lorn song of which the burden was, 'Bleeding Heart, Bleeding Heart, bleeding away,' until she died. It was objected by the murderous party that this Refrain was notoriously the invention of a tambour-worker, a spinster and romantic, still lodging in the Yard. But, forasmuch as all favourite legends must be associated with the affections, and as many more people fall in love than commit murder – which it may be hoped, howsoever bad we are, will continue until the end of the world to be the dispensation under which we shall live – the Bleeding Heart, Bleeding Heart, bleeding away story, carried the day by a great majority. Neither party would listen to the antiquaries who delivered learned lectures in the neighbourhood, showing the Bleeding Heart to have been the heraldic cognisance of the old family to whom the property had once belonged. And, considering that the hour-glass they turned from year to year was filled with the earthiest and coarsest sand, the Bleeding Heart Yarders had reason enough for objecting to be despoiled of the one little golden grain of poetry that sparkled in it.

From *Little Dorrit*

From Bleeding Heart Yard, head south to Gray's Inn

HAVING OCCASION TO transact some business with a solicitor who occupies a highly suicidal set of chambers in Gray's Inn, I afterwards took a turn in the large square of that stronghold of Melancholy, reviewing, with congenial surroundings, my experiences of Chambers.

I began, as was natural, with the Chambers I had just left. They were an upper set on a rotten staircase, with a mysterious bunk or bulkhead on the landing outside them, of a rather nautical and Screw Collier-like appearance than otherwise, and painted an intense black. Many dusty years have passed since the appropriation of this Davy Jones's locker to any purpose, and during the whole period within the memory of living man, it has been hasped and padlocked. I cannot quite satisfy my mind whether it was originally meant for the reception of coals, or bodies, or as a place of temporary security for the plunder 'looted' by laundresses; but I incline to the last opinion. It is about breast high, and usually serves as a bulk for defendants in reduced circumstances to lean against and ponder at, when they come on the hopeful errand of trying to make an arrangement without money – under which auspicious circumstances it mostly happens that the legal gentleman they want to see, is much engaged, and they pervade the staircase for a considerable period. Against this opposing bulk, in the absurdest manner, the tomb-like outer door of the solicitor's chambers (which is also of an intense black) stands in dark ambush, half open, and half shut, all day. The solicitor's apartments are three in number; consisting of a slice, a cell, and a wedge. The slice is assigned to the two clerks, the cell is occupied by the principal, and the wedge is devoted to stray papers, old game baskets from the country, a washing-stand, and a model of a patent Ship's Caboose which was exhibited in Chancery at the commencement of the present century on an application for an injunction to restrain infringement. At about half-past nine on every weekday morning, the younger of the two clerks (who, I have reason to believe, leads the fashion at Pentonville in the articles of pipes and shirts) may be found knocking the dust out of his official door-key on the bunk or locker before mentioned; and so exceedingly subject to dust is his key, and so very retentive of that superfluity, that in exceptional summer weather when a ray of sunlight has fallen on the locker in my presence, I have noticed its inexpressive countenance to be deeply marked by a kind of Bramah erysipelas or small-pox.

This set of chambers (as I have gradually discovered, when I have had restless occasion to make inquiries or leave messages, after office hours) is under the charge of a lady named Sweeney, in figure extremely like an old family-umbrella: whose dwelling confronts a dead wall in a court off Gray's Inn-lane, and who is usually fetched into the passage of that bower, when wanted, from some neighbouring home of industry, which has the curious property of imparting an inflammatory appearance to her visage. Mrs Sweeney is one of the race of professed laundresses, and is the compiler of a remarkable manuscript volume entitled 'Mrs Sweeney's Book,' from which much curious statistical information may be gathered respecting the high prices and small uses of soda, soap, sand, firewood, and other such articles. I have created a legend in my mind – and consequently I believe it with the utmost pertinacity – that the late Mr Sweeney was a ticket-porter under the Honourable Society of Gray's Inn, and that, in consideration of his long and valuable services, Mrs Sweeney was appointed to her present post. For, though devoid of personal charms, I have observed this lady to exercise a fascination over the elderly ticket-porter mind (particularly under the gateway, and in corners and entries), which I can only refer to her being one of the fraternity, yet not competing with it. All that need be said concerning this set of chambers, is said, when I have added that it is in a large double house in Gray's Inn-square, very much out of repair, and that the outer portal is ornamented in a hideous manner with certain stone remains, which have the appearance of the dismembered bust, torso, and limbs of a petrified bencher.

Indeed, I look upon Gray's Inn generally as one of the most depressing institutions in brick and mortar, known to the children of men. Can anything be more dreary than its arid Square, Sahara Desert of the law, with the ugly old tiled-topped tenements, the dirty windows, the bills To Let, To Let, the door-posts inscribed like gravestones, the crazy gateway giving upon the filthy Lane, the scowling, iron-barred prison-like passage into Verulam-buildings, the mouldy red-nosed ticket-porters with little coffin plates, and why with aprons, the dry, hard, atomy-like appearance of the whole dust-heap? When my uncommercial travels tend to this dismal spot, my comfort is its rickety state. Imagination gloats over the fulness of time when the staircases shall have quite tumbled down – they are daily wearing into an ill-savoured powder, but have not quite tumbled down yet – when the last old prolix bencher all of the olden time, shall have been got out of an upper window by means of a Fire Ladder, and carried off to the Holborn Union; when the last clerk shall have engrossed the last parchment behind the last splash on the last of the mud-stained windows, which, all through the miry year, are pilloried out of recognition in Gray's Inn-lane. Then, shall a squalid little trench, with rank grass and a pump in it, lying between the coffee-house and South-square, be wholly given up to cats and rats, and not, as now, have its empire divided between those animals and a few briefless bipeds – surely called to the Bar by voices of deceiving spirits, seeing that they are wanted there by no mortal – who glance down, with eyes better glazed than their casements, from their dreary and lacklustre rooms. Then shall the way Nor' Westward, now lying under a short grim colonnade where in summer-time pounce flies from law-stationering windows into the eyes of laymen, be choked with rubbish and happily become impassable.

From *The Uncommercial Traveller*

From Gray's Inn to Lincoln's Inn

LONDON. MICHAELMAS TERM lately over, and the Lord Chancellor sitting in Lincoln's Inn Hall. Implacable November weather. As much mud in the streets as if the waters had but newly retired from the face of the earth, and it would not be wonderful to meet a Megalosaurus, forty feet long or so, waddling like an elephantine lizard up Holborn Hill. Smoke lowering down from chimney-pots, making a soft black drizzle, with flakes of soot in it as big as full-grown snowflakes – gone into mourning, one might imagine, for the death of the sun. Dogs, undistinguishable in mire. Horses, scarcely better; splashed to their very blinkers. Foot passengers, jostling one another's umbrellas in a general infection of ill temper, and losing their foot-hold at street-corners, where tens of thousands of other foot passengers have been slipping and sliding since the day broke (if this day ever broke), adding new deposits to the crust upon crust of mud, sticking at those points tenaciously to the pavement, and accumulating at compound interest.

Fog everywhere. Fog up the river, where it flows among green aits and meadows; fog down the river, where it rolls defiled among the tiers of shipping and the waterside pollutions of a great (and dirty) city. Fog on the Essex marshes, fog on the Kentish heights. Fog creeping into the cabooses of collier-brigs; fog lying out on the yards and hovering in the rigging of great ships; fog drooping on the gunwales of barges and small boats. Fog in the eyes and throats of ancient Greenwich pensioners, wheezing by the firesides of their wards; fog in the stem and bowl of the afternoon pipe of the wrathful skipper, down in his close cabin; fog cruelly pinching the toes and fingers of his shivering little 'prentice boy on deck. Chance people on the bridges peeping over the parapets into a nether sky of fog, with fog all round them, as if they were up in a balloon and hanging in the misty clouds.

Gas looming through the fog in divers places in the streets, much as the sun may, from the spongey fields, be seen to loom by husbandman and ploughboy. Most of the shops lighted two hours before their time – as the gas seems to know, for it has a haggard and unwilling look.

The raw afternoon is rawest, and the dense fog is densest, and the muddy streets are muddiest near that leaden-headed old obstruction, appropriate ornament for the threshold of a leaden-headed old corporation, Temple Bar. And hard by Temple Bar, in Lincoln's Inn Hall, at the very heart of the fog, sits the Lord High Chancellor in his High Court of Chancery.

From *Bleak House*

From Lincoln's Inn to the Old Curiosity Shop, with Little Nell

CLAPPING HER HANDS with pleasure and running on before me for a short distance, my little acquaintance stopped at a door and remaining on the step till I came up knocked at it when I joined her.

A part of this door was of glass unprotected by any shutter, which I did not observe at first, for all was very dark and silent within, and I was anxious (as indeed the child was also) for an answer to our summons. When she had knocked twice or thrice there was a noise as if some person were moving inside, and at length a faint light appeared through the glass which, as it approached very slowly, the bearer having to make his way through a great many scattered articles, enabled me to see both what kind of person it was who advanced and what kind of place it was through which he came.

It was an old man with long grey hair, whose face

and figure as he held the light above his head and looked before him as he approached, I could plainly see. Though much altered by age, I fancied I could recognize in his spare and slender form something of that delicate mould which I had noticed in a child. Their bright blue eyes were certainly alike, but his face was so deeply furrowed and so very full of care, that here all resemblance ceased.

The place through which he made his way at leisure was one of those receptacles for old and curious things which seem to crouch in odd corners of this town and to hide their musty treasures from the public eye in jealousy and distrust. There were suits of mail standing like ghosts in armour here and there, fantastic carvings brought from monkish cloisters, rusty weapons of various kinds, distorted figures in china and wood and iron and ivory: tapestry and strange furniture that might have been designed in dreams. The haggard aspect of the little old man was wonderfully suited to the place; he might have groped among old churches and tombs and deserted houses and gathered all the spoils with his own hands. There was nothing in the whole collection but was in keeping with himself; nothing that looked older or more worn than he.

As he turned the key in the lock, he surveyed me with some astonishment which was not diminished when he looked from me to my companion.

The door being opened, the child addressed him as grandfather, and told him the little story of our companionship.

'Why, bless thee, child,' said the old man, patting her on the head, 'how couldst thou miss thy way? What if I had lost thee, Nell!'

'I would have found my way back to *you*, grandfather,' said the child boldly; 'never fear.'

The old man kissed her, then turning to me and begging me to walk in, I did so. The door was closed and locked.

From *The Old Curiosity Shop*

From Portsmouth Street*, head west to Seven Dials

THE STRANGER WHO finds himself in 'The Dials' for the first time, and stands Belzoni-like, at the entrance of seven obscure passages, uncertain which to take, will see enough around him to keep his curiosity and attention awake for no inconsiderable time. From the irregular square into which he has plunged, the streets and courts dart in all directions, until they are lost in the unwholesome vapour which hangs over the house-tops, and renders the dirty perspective uncertain and confined; and lounging at every

* Site of a Grade II listed building reputed to be the oldest shop in London and the inspiration for the 'Old Curiosity Shop'. However, Dickens himself writes at the end of his novel that 'The old house had been long ago pulled down, and a fine broad road was in its place.' Other potential sites for the Old Curiosity Shop are Orange Street or Fetter Lane.

corner, as if they came there to take a few gasps of such fresh air as has found its way so far, but is too much exhausted already, to be enabled to force itself into the narrow alleys around, are groups of people, whose appearance and dwellings would fill any mind but a regular Londoner's with astonishment.

On one side, a little crowd has collected round a couple of ladies, who having imbibed the contents of various 'three-outs' of gin and bitters in the course of the morning, have at length differed on some point of domestic arrangement, and are on the eve of settling the quarrel satisfactorily, by an appeal to blows, greatly to the interest of other ladies who live in the same house, and tenements adjoining, and who are all partisans on one side or other.

'Vy don't you pitch into her, Sarah?' exclaims one half-dressed matron, by way of encouragement. 'Vy don't you? if *my* 'usband had treated her with a drain last night, unbeknown to me, I'd tear her precious eyes out – a wixen!'

'What's the matter, ma'am?' inquires another old woman, who has just bustled up to the spot.

'Matter!' replies the first speaker, talking *at* the obnoxious combatant, 'matter! Here's poor dear Mrs Sulliwin, as has five blessed children of her own, can't go out a charing for one arternoon, but what hussies must be a comin', and 'ticing avay her oun' 'usband, as she's been married to twelve year come next Easter Monday, for I see the certificate ven I vas a drinkin' a cup o' tea vith her, only the werry last blessed Ven'sday as ever was sent. I 'appen'd to say promiscuously, "Mrs Sulliwin," says I –'

'What do you mean by hussies?' interrupts a champion of the other party, who has evinced a strong inclination throughout to get up a branch fight on her own account ('Hooroar,' ejaculates a pot-boy in parenthesis, 'put the kye-bosk on her, Mary!'), 'What do you mean by hussies?' reiterates the champion.

'Niver mind,' replies the opposition expressively, 'niver mind; *you* go home, and, ven you're quite sober, mend your stockings.'

This somewhat personal allusion, not only to the lady's habits of intemperance, but also to the state of her wardrobe, rouses her utmost ire, and she accordingly complies with the urgent request of the bystanders to 'pitch in,' with considerable alacrity. The scuffle became general, and terminates, in minor play-bill phraseology, with 'arrival of the policemen, interior of the station-house, and impressive *dénouement*.'

In addition to the numerous groups who are idling about the gin-shops and squabbling in the centre of the road, every post in the open space has its occupant, who leans against it for hours, with listless perseverance. It is odd enough that one class of men in London appear to have no enjoyment beyond leaning against posts. We never saw a regular brick-layer's labourer take any other recreation, fighting excepted. Pass through St Giles's in the evening of a week-day, there they are in their fustian dresses, spotted with brick-dust and whitewash, leaning against posts. Walk through Seven Dials on Sunday morning: there they are again, drab or light corduroy trousers, Blucher boots, blue coats, and great yellow waistcoats, leaning against posts. The idea of a man dressing himself in his best clothes, to lean against a post all day!

The peculiar character of these streets, and the close resemblance each one bears to its neighbour, by no means tends to decrease the bewilderment in which the unexperienced wayfarer through 'the Dials' finds himself involved. He traverses streets of dirty, straggling houses, with now and then an unexpected court composed of buildings as ill-proportioned and deformed as the half-naked children that wallow in the kennels. Here and there, a little dark chandler's shop, with a cracked bell hung up behind the door to announce the entrance of a customer, or betray the presence of some young gentleman in whom a passion for shop tills has developed itself at an early age: others, as if for support, against some handsome lofty building, which usurps the place of a low dingy public-house; long rows of broken and patched windows expose plants that may have flourished when 'the Dials' were built, in vessels as dirty as 'the Dials' themselves; and shops for the purchase of rags, bones, old iron, and kitchen-stuff, vie in cleanliness with the bird-fanciers and rabbit-dealers, which one might fancy so many arks, but for the irresistible conviction that no bird in its proper senses, who was permitted to leave one of them, would ever come back again. Brokers' shops, which would seem to have been established by humane individuals, as refuges for destitute bugs, interspersed with announcements of day-schools, penny theatres, petition-writers, mangles, and music for balls or routs, complete the 'still life' of the subject; and dirty men, filthy women, squalid children, fluttering shuttlecocks, noisy battledores, reeking pipes, bad fruit, more than doubtful oysters, attenuated cats, depressed dogs, and anatomical fowls, are its cheerful accompaniments.

From *Sketches by Boz*

From Seven Dials to Covent Garden, then down to the river at Waterloo, with Tom Pinch and his sister

HAVING ALWAYS BEEN an early riser and having now no organ to engage him in sweet converse every morning, it was his habit to take a long walk before going to the Temple; and naturally inclining, as a stranger, towards those parts of the town which were conspicuous for the life and animation pervading them, he became a great frequenter of the market-places, bridges, quays, and especially the steam-boat wharves; for it was very lively and fresh to see the people hurrying away upon their many schemes of business or pleasure, and it made Tom glad to think that there was that much change and freedom in the monotonous routine of city lives.

In most of these morning excursions Ruth accompanied him. As their landlord was always up and away at his business (whatever that might be, no one seemed to know) at a very early hour, the habits of the people of the house in which they lodged corresponded with their own. Thus they had often finished their breakfast, and were out in the summer air, by seven o'clock. After a two hours' stroll they parted at some convenient point: Tom going to the Temple, and his sister returning home, as methodically as you please.

Many and many a pleasant stroll they had in Covent Garden Market: snuffing up the perfume of the fruits and flowers, wondering at the magnificence of the pine-apples and melons; catching glimpses down side avenues, of rows and rows of old women, seated on inverted baskets shelling peas; looking unutterable things at the fat bundles of asparagus with which the dainty shops were fortified as with a breastwork; and, at the herbalist's doors, gratefully inhaling scents as of veal-stuffing yet uncooked, dreamily mixed up with capsicums, brown-paper, seeds: even with hints of lusty snails and fine young curly leeches. Many and many a pleasant stroll they had among the poultry markets, where ducks and fowls, with necks unnaturally long, lay stretched out in pairs, ready for cooking; where there were speckled eggs in mossy baskets, white country sausages beyond impeachment by surviving cat or dog, or horse or donkey, new cheeses to any wild extent, live birds in coops and cages, looking much too big to be natural, in consequence of those receptacles being much too little; rabbits, alive and dead, innumerable. Many a pleasant stroll they had among the cool, refreshing, silvery fish-stalls, with a kind of moonlight effect about their stock-in-trade, excepting always for the ruddy lobsters. Many a pleasant stroll among the waggon-loads of fragrant hay, beneath which dogs and tired waggoners lay fast asleep, oblivious of the pieman and the public-house. But never half so good a stroll as down among the steamboats on a bright morning.

There they lay, alongside of each other; hard and fast for ever, to all appearance, but designing to get out somehow, and quite confident of doing it; and in that faith shoals of passengers, and heaps of luggage, were proceeding hurriedly on board. Little steamboats dashed up and down the stream incessantly. Tiers upon tiers of vessels, scores of masts, labyrinths of tackle, idle sails, splashing oars, gliding row-boats, lumbering barges, sunken piles, with ugly lodgings for the water-rat within their mud-discoloured nooks; church steeples, warehouses, house-roofs, arches, bridges, men and women, children, casks, cranes, boxes, horses, coaches, idlers, and hard-labourers: there they were, all jumbled up together, any summer morning, far beyond Tom's power of separation.

In the midst of all this turmoil there was an

incessant roar from every packet's funnel, which quite expressed and carried out the uppermost emotion of the scene. They all appeared to be perspiring and bothering themselves, exactly as their passengers did; they never left off fretting and chafing, in their own hoarse manner, once; but were always panting out, without any stops, 'Come along do make haste I'm very nervous come along oh good gracious we shall never get there how late you are do make haste I'm off directly come along!' Even when they had left off, and had got safely out into the current, on the smallest provocation they began again: for the bravest packet of them all, being stopped by some entanglement in the river, would immediately begin to fume and pant afresh, 'oh here's a stoppage what's the matter do go on there I'm in a hurry it's done on purpose did you ever oh my goodness do go on here!' and so, in a state of mind bordering on distraction, would be last seen drifting slowly through the mist into the summer light beyond, that made it red.

From *Martin Chuzzlewit*

Along the Strand and Fleet Street with David Copperfield

I WAS SO young and childish, and so little qualified – how could I be otherwise? – to undertake the whole charge of my own existence, that often, in going to Murdstone and Grinby's, of a morning, I could not resist the stale pastry put out for sale at half-price at the pastrycooks' doors, and spent in that the money I should have kept for my dinner. Then, I went without my dinner, or bought a roll or a slice of pudding. I remember two pudding shops, between which I was divided, according to my finances. One was in a court close to St Martin's Church – at the back of the church, – which is now removed altogether. The pudding at that shop was made of currants, and was rather a special pudding, but was dear, twopennyworth not being larger than a pennyworth of more ordinary pudding. A good shop for the latter was in the Strand – somewhere in that part which has been rebuilt since. It was a stout pale pudding, heavy and flabby, and with great flat raisins in it, stuck in whole at wide distances apart. It came up hot at about my time every day, and many a day did I dine off it. When I dined regularly and handsomely, I had a saveloy and a penny loaf, or a fourpenny plate of red beef from a cook's shop; or a plate of bread and cheese and a glass of beer, from a miserable old public-house opposite our place of business, called the Lion, or the Lion and something else that I have forgotten. Once, I remember carrying my own bread (which I had brought from home in the morning) under my arm, wrapped in a piece of paper, like a book, and going to a famous alamode beef-house near Drury Lane, and ordering a 'small plate' of that delicacy to eat with it. What the waiter thought of such a strange little apparition coming in all alone, I don't know; but I can see him now, staring at me as I ate my dinner, and bringing up the other waiter to look. I gave him a halfpenny for himself, and I wish he hadn't taken it.

We had half-an-hour, I think, for tea. When I had money enough, I used to get half-a-pint of ready-made coffee and a slice of bread and butter. When I had none, I used to look at a venison shop in Fleet Street; or I have strolled, at such a time, as far as Covent Garden Market, and stared at the pineapples. I was fond of wandering about the Adelphi, because it was a mysterious place, with those dark arches. I see myself emerging one evening from some of these arches, on a little public-house close to the river, with an open space before it, where some coal-heavers were dancing; to look at whom I sat down upon a bench. I wonder what they thought of me!

From *David Copperfield*

From Waterloo, head east to Temple

I WAS THREE-AND-TWENTY years of age. Not another word had I heard to enlighten me on the subject of my expectations, and my twenty-third birthday was a week gone. We had left Barnard's Inn more than a year, and lived in the Temple. Our chambers were in Garden-court, down by the river . . .

Business had taken Herbert on a journey to Marseilles. I was alone, and had a dull sense of being alone. Dispirited and anxious, long hoping that to-morrow or next week would clear my way, and long disappointed, I sadly missed the cheerful face and ready response of my friend.

It was wretched weather; stormy and wet, stormy and wet; and mud, mud, mud, deep in all the streets. Day after day, a vast heavy veil had been driving over London from the East, and it drove still, as if in the East there were an Eternity of cloud and wind. So furious had been the gusts, that high buildings in town had had the lead stripped off their roofs; and in the country, trees had been torn up, and sails of windmills carried away; and gloomy accounts had come in from the coast, of shipwreck and death. Violent blasts of rain had accompanied these rages of wind, and the day just closed as I sat down to read had been the worst of all.

Alterations have been made in that part of the Temple since that time, and it has not now so lonely a character as it had then, nor is it so exposed to the river. We lived at the top of the last house, and the wind rushing up the river shook the house that night, like discharges of cannon, or breakings of a sea. When the rain came with it and dashed against the windows, I thought, raising my eyes to them as they rocked, that I might have fancied myself in a storm-beaten lighthouse. Occasionally, the smoke came rolling down the chimney as though it could not bear to go out into such a night; and when I set the doors open and looked down the staircase, the staircase lamps were blown out; and when I shaded my face with my hands and looked through the black windows (opening them ever so little, was out of the question in the teeth of such wind and rain) I saw that the lamps in the court were blown out, and that the lamps on the bridges and the shore were shuddering, and that the coal fires in barges on the river were being carried away before the wind like red-hot splashes in the rain.

I read with my watch upon the table, purposing to close my book at eleven o'clock. As I shut it, Saint Paul's, and all the many church-clocks in the City – some leading, some accompanying, some following – struck that hour. The sound was curiously flawed by the wind; and I was listening, and thinking how the wind assailed and tore it, when I heard a footstep on the stair.

From *Great Expectations*

From Temple, head North to Snow Hill, to meet Wackford Squeers

Snow Hill! What kind of place can the quiet townspeople who see the words emblazoned, in all the legibility of gilt letters and dark shading, on the north-country coaches, take Snow Hill to be? All people have some undefined and shadowy notion of a place whose name is frequently before their eyes, or often in their ears. What a vast number of random ideas there must be perpetually floating about, regarding this same Snow Hill. The name is such a good one. Snow Hill – Snow Hill too, coupled with a Saracen's Head: picturing to us by a double association of ideas, something stern and rugged! A bleak desolate tract of country, open to piercing blasts and fierce wintry storms – a dark, cold, gloomy heath, lonely by day, and scarcely to be thought of by honest folks at night – a place which solitary wayfarers shun, and where desperate robbers congregate; – this, or something like this, should be the prevalent notion of Snow Hill, in those remote and rustic parts, through which the Saracen's Head, like some grim apparition, rushes each day and night with mysterious and ghost-like punctuality; holding its swift and headlong course in all weathers, and seeming to bid defiance to the very elements themselves.

The reality is rather different, but by no means to be despised notwithstanding. There, at the very core of London, in the heart of its business and animation, in the midst of a whirl of noise and motion: stemming as it were the giant currents of life that flow ceaselessly on from different quarters, and meet beneath its walls: stands Newgate; and in that crowded street on which it frowns so darkly – within a few feet of the squalid tottering houses – upon the very spot on which the vendors of soup and fish and damaged fruit are now plying their trades – scores of human beings, amidst a roar of sounds to which even the tumult of a great city is as nothing, four, six, or eight strong men at a time, have been hurried violently and swiftly from the world, when the scene has been rendered frightful with excess of human life; when curious eyes have glared from casement and house-top, and wall and pillar; and when, in the mass of white and upturned faces, the dying wretch, in his all-comprehensive look of agony, has met not one – not one – that bore the impress of pity or compassion.

Near to the jail, and by consequence near to Smithfield also, and the Compter, and the bustle and noise of the city; and just on that particular part of Snow Hill where omnibus horses going eastward seriously think of falling down on purpose, and where horses in hackney cabriolets going westward not unfrequently fall by accident, is the coach-yard of the Saracen's Head Inn; its portal guarded by two Saracens' heads and shoulders, which it was once the pride and glory of the choice spirits of this metropolis to pull down at night, but which have for some time remained in undisturbed tranquillity; possibly because this species of humour is now confined to St James's parish, where door knockers are preferred as being more portable, and bell-wires esteemed as convenient toothpicks. Whether this be the reason or not, there they are, frowning upon you from each side of the gateway. The inn itself garnished with another Saracen's Head, frowns upon you from the top of the yard; while from the door of the hind boot of all the red coaches that are standing therein, there glares a small Saracen's Head, with a twin expression to the large Saracens' Heads below, so that the general appearance of the pile is decidedly of the Saracenic order.

When you walk up this yard, you will see the

booking-office on your left, and the tower of St Sepulchre's church, darting abruptly up into the sky, on your right, and a gallery of bedrooms on both sides. Just before you, you will observe a long window with the words 'coffee-room' legibly painted above it; and looking out of that window, you would have seen in addition, if you had gone at the right time, Mr Wackford Squeers with his hands in his pockets.

Mr Squeers's appearance was not prepossessing. He had but one eye, and the popular prejudice runs in favour of two. The eye he had, was unquestionably useful, but decidedly not ornamental: being of a greenish grey, and in shape resembling the fanlight of a street door. The blank side of his face was much wrinkled and puckered up, which gave him a very sinister appearance, especially when he smiled, at which times his expression bordered closely on the villainous. His hair was very flat and shiny, save at the ends, where it was brushed stiffly up from a low protruding forehead, which assorted well with his harsh voice and coarse manner. He was about two or three and fifty, and a trifle below the middle size; he wore a white neckerchief with long ends, and a suit of scholastic black; but his coat sleeves being a great deal too long, and his trousers a great deal too short, he appeared ill at ease in his clothes, and as if he were in a perpetual state of astonishment at finding himself so respectable.

Mr Squeers was standing in a box by one of the coffee-room fire-places, fitted with one such table as is usually seen in coffee-rooms, and two of extraordinary shapes and dimensions made to suit the angles of the partition. In a corner of the seat, was a very small deal trunk, tied round with a scanty piece of cord; and on the trunk was perched – his lace-up half-boots and corduroy trousers dangling in the air – a diminutive boy, with his shoulders drawn up to his ears, and his hands planted on his knees, who glanced timidly at the schoolmaster, from time to time, with evident dread and apprehension.

'Half-past three,' muttered Mr Squeers, turning from the window, and looking sulkily at the coffee-room clock. 'There will be nobody here today.'

Much vexed by this reflection, Mr Squeers looked at the little boy to see whether he was doing anything he could beat him for. As he happened not to be doing anything at all, he merely boxed his ears, and told him not to do it again.

'At Midsummer,' muttered Mr Squeers, resuming his complaint, 'I took down ten boys; ten twenties is two hundred pound. I go back at eight o'clock tomorrow morning, and have got only three – three oughts is an ought – three twos is six – sixty pound. What's come of all the boys? what's parents got in their heads? what does it all mean?'

Here the little boy on the top of the trunk gave a violent sneeze.

'Halloa, sir!' growled the schoolmaster, turning round. 'What's that, sir?'

'Nothing, please sir,' replied the little boy.

'Nothing, sir!' exclaimed Mr Squeers.

'Please sir, I sneezed,' rejoined the boy, trembling till the little trunk shook under him.

'Oh! sneezed, did you?' retorted Mr Squeers. 'Then what did you say "nothing" for, sir?'

In default of a better answer to this question, the little boy screwed a couple of knuckles into each of his eyes and began to cry, wherefore Mr Squeers knocked him off the trunk with a blow on one side of the face, and knocked him on again with a blow on the other.

'Wait till I get you down into Yorkshire, my young gentleman,' said Mr Squeers, 'and then I'll give you the rest. Will you hold that noise, sir?'

'Ye – ye – yes,' sobbed the little boy, rubbing his face very hard with the Beggar's Petition in printed calico.

'Then do so at once, sir,' said Squeers. 'Do you hear?'

As this admonition was accompanied with a threatening gesture, and uttered with a savage aspect, the little boy rubbed his face harder, as if to keep the tears back; and, beyond alternately sniffing and choking, gave no further vent to his emotions.

From *Nicholas Nickleby*

From Snow Hill, head south again to the Old Bailey

THE ENTRANCE OF the Judge, and a consequent great stir and settling down in the court, stopped the dialogue. Presently, the dock became the central point of interest. Two gaolers, who had been standing there, went out, and the prisoner was brought in, and put to the bar.

Everybody present, except the one wigged gentleman who looked at the ceiling, stared at him. All the human breath in the place, rolled at him, like a sea, or a wind, or a fire. Eager faces strained round pillars and corners, to get a sight of him; spectators in back rows stood up, not to miss a hair of him; people on the floor of the court, laid their hands on the shoulders of the people before them, to help themselves, at anybody's cost, to a view of him – stood a-tiptoe, got upon ledges, stood upon next to nothing, to see every inch of him. Conspicuous among these latter, like an animated bit of the spiked wall of Newgate, Jerry stood: aiming at the prisoner the beery breath of a whet he had taken as he came along, and discharging it to mingle with the waves of other beer, and gin, and tea, and coffee, and what not, that flowed at him, and already broke upon the great windows behind him in an impure mist and rain.

The object of all this staring and blaring, was a young man of about five-and-twenty, well-grown and well-looking, with a sunburnt cheek and a dark eye. His condition was that of a young gentleman. He was plainly dressed in black, or very dark grey, and his hair, which was long and dark, was gathered in a ribbon at the back of his neck; more to be out of his way than for ornament. As an emotion of the mind will express itself through any covering of the body, so the paleness which his situation engendered came through the brown upon his cheek, showing the soul to be stronger than the sun. He was otherwise quite self-possessed, bowed to the Judge, and stood quiet.

The sort of interest with which this man was stared and breathed at, was not a sort that elevated humanity. Had he stood in peril of a less horrible sentence – had there been a chance of any one of its savage details being spared – by just so much would he have lost in his fascination. The form that was to be doomed to be so shamefully mangled, was the sight; the immortal creature that was to be so butchered and torn asunder, yielded the sensation. Whatever gloss the various spectators put upon the interest, according to their several arts and powers of self-deceit, the interest was, at the root of it, Ogreish.

Silence in the court! Charles Darnay had yesterday pleaded Not Guilty to an indictment denouncing him (with infinite jingle and jangle) for that he was a false traitor to our serene, illustrious, excellent, and so forth, prince, our Lord the King, by reason of his having, on divers occasions, and by divers means and ways, assisted Lewis, the French King, in his wars against our said serene, illustrious, excellent, and so forth; that was to say, by coming and going, between the dominions of our said serene, illustrious, excellent, and so forth, and those of the said French Lewis, and wickedly, falsely, traitorously, and otherwise evil-adverbiously, revealing to the said French Lewis what forces our said serene, illustrious, excellent, and so forth, had in preparation to send to Canada and North America. This much, Jerry, with his head becoming more and more spiky as the law terms bristled it, made out with huge satisfaction, and so arrived circuitously at the understanding that the aforesaid, and over and over again aforesaid, Charles Darnay, stood there before him upon his trial; that the jury were swearing in; and that Mr Attorney-General was making ready to speak.

The accused, who was (and who knew he was) being mentally hanged, beheaded, and quartered, by everybody there, neither flinched from the situation, nor assumed any theatrical air in it. He was quiet and attentive; watched the opening proceedings with a grave interest; and stood with his hands resting on the slab of wood before him, so composedly, that they had not displaced a leaf of the herbs with which it was strewn. The court was all bestrewn with herbs and sprinkled with vinegar, as a precaution against gaol air and gaol fever.

Over the prisoner's head there was a mirror, to throw the light down upon him. Crowds of the wicked and the wretched had been reflected in it, and had passed from its surface and this earth's together. Haunted in a most ghastly manner that abominable place would have been, if the glass could ever have rendered back its reflections, as the ocean is one day to give up its dead. Some passing thought of the infamy and disgrace for which it had been reserved, may have struck the prisoner's mind. Be that as it may, a change in his position making him conscious of a bar of light across his face, he looked up; and when he saw the glass his face flushed, and his right hand pushed the herbs away.

From A *Tale of Two Cities*

From the Old Bailey down to Ludgate Hill

It was a Sunday evening in London, gloomy, close, and stale. Maddening church bells of all degrees of dissonance, sharp and flat, cracked and clear, fast and slow, made the brick-and-mortar echoes hideous. Melancholy streets, in a penitential garb of soot, steeped the souls of the people who were condemned to look at them out of windows, in dire despondency. In every thoroughfare, up almost every alley, and down almost every turning, some doleful bell was throbbing, jerking, tolling, as if the Plague were in the city and the dead-carts were going round. Everything was bolted and barred that could by possibility furnish relief to an overworked people. No pictures, no unfamiliar animals, no rare plants or flowers, no natural or artificial wonders of the ancient world – all taboo with that enlightened strictness, that the ugly South Sea gods in the British Museum might have supposed themselves at home again. Nothing to see but streets, streets, streets. Nothing to breathe but streets, streets, streets. Nothing to change the brooding mind, or raise it up. Nothing for the spent toiler to do, but to compare the monotony of his seventh day with the monotony of his six days, think what a weary life he led, and make the best of it – or the worst, according to the probabilities.

At such a happy time, so propitious to the interests of religion and morality, Mr Arthur Clennam, newly arrived from Marseilles by way of Dover, and by Dover coach the Blue-eyed Maid, sat in the window of a coffee-house on Ludgate Hill. Ten thousand responsible houses surrounded him, frowning as heavily on the streets they composed, as if they were every one inhabited by the ten young men of the Calender's story, who blackened their faces and bemoaned their miseries every night. Fifty thousand lairs surrounded him where people lived so unwholesomely that fair water put into their crowded rooms on Saturday night, would be corrupt on Sunday morning; albeit my lord, their county member, was amazed that they failed to sleep in company with their butcher's meat. Miles of close wells and pits of houses, where the inhabitants gasped for air, stretched far away towards every point of the compass. Through the heart of the town a deadly sewer ebbed and flowed, in the place of a fine fresh river. What secular want could the million or so of human beings whose daily labour, six days in the week, lay among these Arcadian objects, from the sweet sameness of which they had no escape between the cradle and the grave – what secular want could they possibly have upon their seventh day? Clearly they could want nothing but a stringent policeman.

Mr Arthur Clennam sat in the window of the coffee-house on Ludgate Hill, counting one of the neighbouring bells, making sentences and burdens of songs out of it in spite of himself, and wondering how many sick people it might be the death of in the course of the year. As the hour approached, its changes of measure made it more and more exasperating. At the quarter, it went off into a condition of deadly-lively importunity, urging the populace in a voluble manner to Come to church, Come to church, Come to church! At the ten minutes, it became aware that the congregation would be scanty, and slowly hammered out in low spirits, They WON'T come, they WON'T come, they WON'T come! At the five minutes, it abandoned hope, and shook every house in the neighbourhood for three hundred seconds, with one dismal swing per second, as a groan of despair.

'Thank Heaven!' said Clennam, when the hour struck, and the bell stopped.

*

He sat in the same place as the day died, looking at the dull houses opposite, and thinking, if the disembodied spirits of former inhabitants were ever conscious of them, how they must pity themselves for their old places of imprisonment. Sometimes a face would appear behind the dingy glass of a window, and would fade away into the gloom as if it had seen enough of life and had vanished out of it. Presently the rain began to fall in slanting lines between him and those houses, and people began to collect under cover of the public passage opposite, and to look out hopelessly at the sky as the rain dropped thicker and faster. Then wet umbrellas began to appear, draggled skirts, and mud. What the mud had been doing with itself, or where it came from, who could say? But it seemed to collect in a moment, as a crowd will, and in five minutes to have splashed all the sons and daughters of Adam. The lamplighter was going his rounds now; and as the fiery jets sprang up under his touch, one might have fancied them astonished at being suffered to introduce any show of brightness into such a dismal scene.

Mr Arthur Clennam took up his hat and buttoned his coat, and walked out. In the country, the rain would have developed a thousand fresh scents, and every drop would have had its bright association with some beautiful form of growth or life. In the city, it developed only foul stale smells, and was a sickly, lukewarm, dirt-stained, wretched addition to the gutters.

From *Little Dorrit*

From Ludgate Hill to St Paul's Cathedral

I PAID MY fee of twopence upon entering, to one of the money-changers who sit within the Temple; and falling, after a few turns up and down, into the quiet train of thought which such a place awakens, paced the echoing stones like some old monk whose present world lay all within its walls. As I looked afar up into the lofty dome, I could not help wondering what were his reflections whose genius reared that mighty pile, when, the last small wedge of timber fixed, the last nail driven into its home for many centuries, the clang of hammers, and the hum of busy voices gone, and the Great Silence whole years of noise had helped to make, reigning undisturbed around, he mused, as I did now, upon his work, and lost himself amid its vast extent. I could not quite determine whether the contemplation of it would impress him with a sense of greatness or of insignificance; but when I remembered how long a time it had taken to erect, in how short a space it might be traversed even to its remotest parts, for how brief a term he, or any of those who cared to bear his name, would live to see it, or know of its existence, I imagined him far more melancholy than proud, and looking with regret upon his labour done. With these thoughts in my mind, I began to ascend, almost unconsciously, the flight of steps leading to the several wonders of the building, and found myself before a barrier where another money-taker sat, who demanded which among them I would choose to see. There were the stone gallery, he said, and the whispering gallery, the geometrical staircase, the room of models, the clock – the clock being quite in my way, I stopped him there, and chose that sight from all the rest.

I groped my way into the Turret which it occupies, and saw before me, in a kind of loft, what seemed to be a great, old oaken press with folding doors. These being thrown back by the attendant (who was sleeping when I came upon him, and looked a drowsy fellow, as though his close companionship with Time had made him quite indifferent to it), disclosed a complicated crowd of wheels and chains in iron and brass, – great, sturdy, rattling engines, – suggestive of breaking a finger put in here or there, and grinding the bone to powder, – and these were the Clock! Its very pulse, if I may use the word, was like no other clock. It did not mark the flight of every moment with a gentle second stroke, as though it would check old Time, and have him stay his pace in pity, but measured it with one sledge-hammer beat, as if its business were to crush the seconds as they came trooping on, and remorselessly to clear a path before the Day of Judgment.

I sat down opposite to it, and hearing its regular and never-changing voice, that one deep constant note, uppermost amongst all the noise and clatter in the streets below, – marking that, let that tumult rise or fall, go on or stop, – let it be night or noon, to-morrow or to-day, this year or next, – it still performed its functions with the same dull constancy, and regulated the progress of the life around, the fancy came upon me that this was London's Heart, – and that when it should cease to beat, the City would be no more.

It is night. Calm and unmoved amidst the scenes that darkness favours, the great heart of London throbs in its Giant breast. Wealth and beggary, vice and virtue, guilt and innocence, repletion and the direst hunger, all treading on each other and crowding together, are gathered round it. Draw but a little circle above the clustering housetops, and you shall have within its space everything, with its opposite extreme and contradiction, close beside. Where yonder feeble light is shining, a man is but this moment dead. The taper at a few yards' distance is seen by eyes that have this instant opened on the world.

There are two houses separated by but an inch or two of wall. In one, there are quiet minds at rest; in the other, a waking conscience that one might think would trouble the very air. In that close corner where the roofs shrink down and cower together as if to hide their secrets from the handsome street hard by, there are such dark crimes, such miseries and horrors, as could be hardly told in whispers. In the handsome street, there are folks asleep who have dwelt there all their lives, and have no more knowledge of these things than if they had never been, or were transacted at the remotest limits of the world, – who, if they were hinted at, would shake their heads, look wise, and frown, and say they were impossible, and out of Nature, – as if all great towns were not. Does not this Heart of London, that nothing moves, nor stops, nor quickens, – that goes on the same let what will be done, does it not express the City's character well?

The day begins to break, and soon there is the hum and noise of life. Those who have spent the night on doorsteps and cold stones crawl off to beg; they who have slept in beds come forth to their occupation, too, and business is astir. The fog of sleep rolls slowly off, and London shines awake. The streets are filled with carriages and people gaily clad. The jails are full, too, to the throat, nor have the workhouses or hospitals much room to spare. The courts of law are crowded.

Taverns have their regular frequenters by this time, and every mart of traffic has its throng. Each of these places is a world, and has its own inhabitants; each is distinct from, and almost unconscious of the existence of any other. There are some few people well to do, who remember to have heard it said, that numbers of men and women – thousands, they think it was – get up in London every day, unknowing where to lay their heads at night; and that there are quarters of the town where misery and famine always are. They don't believe it quite, – there may be some truth in it, but it is exaggerated, of course. So, each of these thousand worlds goes on, intent upon itself, until night comes again, – first with its lights and pleasures, and its cheerful streets; then with its guilt and darkness.

Heart of London, there is a moral in thy every stroke! As I look on at thy indomitable working, which neither death, nor press of life, nor grief, nor gladness out of doors will influence one jot, I seem to hear a voice within thee which sinks into my heart, bidding me, as I elbow my way among the crowd, have some thought for the meanest wretch that passes, and, being a man, to turn away with scorn and pride from none that bear the human shape.

From *Master Humphrey's Clock*

From St Paul's, down to the river again

IN THESE TIMES of ours, though concerning the exact year there is no need to be precise, a boat of dirty and disreputable appearance, with two figures in it, floated on the Thames, between Southwark bridge which is of iron, and London Bridge which is of stone, as an autumn evening was closing in.

The figures in this boat were those of a strong man with ragged grizzled hair and a sun-browned face, and a dark girl of nineteen or twenty, sufficiently like him to be recognizable as his daughter. The girl rowed, pulling a pair of sculls very easily; the man, with the rudder-lines slack in his hands, and his hands loose in his waistband, kept an eager look out. He had no net, hook, or line, and he could not be a fisherman; his boat had no cushion for a sitter, no paint, no inscription, no appliance beyond a rusty boathook and a coil of rope, and he could not be a waterman; his boat was too crazy and too small to take in cargo for delivery, and he could not be a lighterman or river-carrier; there was no clue to what he looked for, but he looked for something, with a most intent and searching gaze. The tide, which had turned an hour before, was running down, and his eyes watched every little race and eddy in its broad sweep, as the boat made slight head-way against it, or drove stern foremost before it, according as he directed his daughter by a movement of his head. She watched his face as earnestly as he watched the river. But, in the intensity of her look there was a touch of dread or horror.

Allied to the bottom of the river rather than the surface, by reason of the slime and ooze with which it was covered, and its sodden state, this boat and the two figures in it obviously were doing something that they often did, and were seeking what they often sought. Half savage as the man showed, with no covering on his matted head, with his brown arms bare to between the elbow and the shoulder, with the loose knot of a looser kerchief lying low on his bare breast in a wilderness of beard and whisker, with such dress as he wore seeming to be made out of the mud that begrimed his boat, still there was a business-like usage in his steady gaze. So with every lithe action of the girl, with every turn of her wrist, perhaps most of all with her look of dread or horror; they were things of usage.

'Keep her out, Lizzie. Tide runs strong here. Keep her well afore the sweep of it.'

Trusting to the girl's skill and making no use of the rudder, he eyed the coming tide with an absorbed attention. So the girl eyed him. But, it happened now, that a slant of light from the setting sun glanced into the bottom of the boat, and, touching a rotten stain there which bore some resemblance to the outline of a muffled human form, coloured it as though with diluted blood. This caught the girl's eye, and she shivered.

'What ails you?' said the man, immediately aware of it, though so intent on the advancing waters; 'I see nothing afloat.'

The red light was gone, the shudder was gone, and his gaze, which had come back to the boat for a moment, travelled away again. Wheresoever the strong tide met with an impediment, his gaze paused for an instant. At every mooring-chain and rope, at every stationary boat or barge that split the current into a broad arrowhead, at the offsets from the piers of Southwark Bridge, at the paddles of the river steamboats as they beat the filthy water, at the floating logs of timber lashed together lying off certain wharves, his shining eyes darted a hungry look. After a darkening hour or so, suddenly the rudder-lines tightened in his hold, and he steered hard towards the Surrey shore.

Always watching his face, the girl instantly answered to the action in her sculling; presently the boat swung round, quivered as from a sudden jerk, and the upper half of the man was stretched out over the stern.

The girl pulled the hood of a cloak she wore, over her head and over her face, and, looking backward so that the front folds of this hood were turned down the river, kept the boat in that direction going before the tide. Until now, the boat had barely held her own, and had hovered about one spot; but now, the banks changed swiftly, and the deepening shadows and the kindling lights of London Bridge were passed, and the tiers of shipping lay on either hand.

It was not until now that the upper half of the man came back into the boat. His arms were wet and dirty, and he washed them over the side. In his right hand he held something, and he washed that in the river too. It was money. He chinked it once, and he blew upon it once, and he spat upon it once – 'for luck,' he hoarsely said – before he put it in his pocket.

'Lizzie!'

The girl turned her face towards him with a start, and rowed in silence. Her face was very pale. He was a hook-nosed man, and with that and his bright eyes and his ruffled head, bore a certain likeness to a roused bird of prey.

'Take that thing off your face.'

She put it back.

'Here! and give me hold of the sculls. I'll take the rest of the spell.'

'No, no, Father! No! I can't indeed. Father! – I cannot sit so near it!'

He was moving towards her to change places, but her terrified expostulation stopped him and he resumed his seat.

'What hurt can it do you?'

'None, none. But I cannot bear it.'

'It's my belief you hate the sight of the very river.'

'I – I do not like it, Father.'

'As if it wasn't your living! As if it wasn't meat and drink to you!'

At these latter words the girl shivered again, and for a moment paused in her rowing, seeming to turn deadly faint. It escaped his attention, for he was glancing over the stern at something the boat had in tow.

'How can you be so thankless to your best friend, Lizzie? The very fire that warmed you when you were a babby, was picked out of the river alongside the coal barges. The very basket that you slept in, the tide washed ashore. The very rockers that I put it upon to make a cradle of it, I cut out of a piece of wood that drifted from some ship or another.'

Lizzie took her right hand from the scull it held,

and touched her lips with it, and for a moment held it out lovingly towards him: then, without speaking, she resumed her rowing.

From *Our Mutual Friend*

From London Bridge to the Borough, to meet Sam Weller

THERE ARE IN London several old inns, once the headquarters of celebrated coaches in the days when coaches performed their journeys in a graver and more solemn manner than they do in these times; but which have now degenerated into little more than the abiding and booking-places of country waggons. The reader would look in vain for any of these ancient hostelries, among the Golden Crosses and Bull and Mouths, which rear their stately fronts in the improved streets of London. If he would light upon any of these old places, he must direct his steps to the obscurer quarters of the town, and there in some secluded nooks he will find several, still standing with a kind of gloomy sturdiness, amidst the modern innovations which surround them.

In the Borough especially, there still remain some half-dozen old inns, which have preserved their external features unchanged, and which have escaped alike the rage for public improvement and the encroachments of private speculation. Great, rambling queer old places they are, with galleries, and passages, and staircases, wide enough and antiquated enough to furnish materials for a hundred ghost stories, supposing we should ever be reduced to the lamentable necessity of inventing any, and that the world should exist long enough to exhaust the innumerable veracious legends connected with old London Bridge, and its adjacent neighbourhood on the Surrey side.

It was in the yard of one of these inns – of no less celebrated a one than the White Hart – that a man was busily employed in brushing the dirt off a pair of boots, early on the morning succeeding the events narrated in the last chapter. He was habited in a coarse, striped waistcoat, with black calico sleeves, and blue glass buttons; drab breeches and leggings. A bright red handkerchief was wound in a very loose and unstudied style round his neck, and an old white hat was carelessly thrown on one side of his head. There were two rows of boots before him, one cleaned and the other dirty, and at every addition he made to the clean row, he paused from his work, and contemplated its results with evident satisfaction.

The yard presented none of that bustle and activity which are the usual characteristics of a large coach inn. Three or four lumbering wagons, each with a pile of goods beneath its ample canopy, about the height of the second-floor window of an ordinary house, were stowed away beneath a lofty roof which extended over one end of the yard; and another, which was probably to commence its journey that morning, was drawn out into the open space. A double tier of bedroom galleries, with old clumsy balustrades, ran round two sides of the straggling area, and a double row of bells to correspond, sheltered from the weather by a little sloping roof, hung over the door leading to the bar and coffee-room. Two or three gigs and chaise-carts were wheeled up under different little sheds and pent-houses; and the occasional heavy tread of a cart-horse, or rattling of a chain at the farther end of the yard, announced to anybody who cared about the matter, that the stable lay in that direction. When we add that a few boys in smock-frocks were lying asleep on heavy packages, wool-packs, and other articles that were scattered about on heaps of straw, we have described as fully as need be the general appearance of the yard of the White Hart Inn, High Street, Borough, on the particular morning in question.

A loud ringing of one of the bells was followed by the appearance of a smart chambermaid in the upper sleeping gallery, who, after tapping at one of the doors, and receiving a request from within, called over the balustrades – 'Sam!'

'Hollo,' replied the man with the white hat.

'Number twenty-two wants his boots.'

'Ask number twenty-two, vether he'll have 'em now, or vait till he gets 'em,' was the reply.

'Come, don't be a fool, Sam,' said the girl coaxingly, 'the gentleman wants his boots directly.'

'Well, you ARE a nice young 'ooman for a musical party, you are,' said the boot-cleaner. 'Look at these here boots – eleven pair o' boots; and one shoe as belongs to number six, with the wooden leg. The eleven boots is to be called at half-past eight and the shoe at nine. Who's number twenty-two, that's to put all the others out? No, no; reg'lar rotation, as Jack Ketch said, ven he tied the men up. Sorry to keep you a-waitin', Sir, but I'll attend to you directly.'

Saying which, the man in the white hat set to work upon a top-boot with increased assiduity.

There was another loud ring; and the bustling old landlady of the White Hart made her appearance in the opposite gallery.

'Sam,' cried the landlady, 'where's that lazy, idle – why, Sam – oh, there you are; why don't you answer?'

'Vouldn't be gen-teel to answer, till you'd done talking,' replied Sam gruffly.

'Here, clean these shoes for number seventeen directly, and take 'em to private sitting-room, number five, first floor.'

The landlady flung a pair of lady's shoes into the yard, and bustled away.

'Number five,' said Sam, as he picked up the shoes, and taking a piece of chalk from his pocket, made a memorandum of their destination on the soles – 'Lady's shoes and private sittin'-room! I suppose she didn't come in the vagin.'

'She came in early this morning,' cried the girl, who was still leaning over the railing of the gallery, 'with a gentleman in a hackney-coach, and it's him as wants his boots, and you'd better do 'em, that's all about it.'

'Vy didn't you say so before,' said Sam, with great indignation, singling out the boots in question from the heap before him. 'For all I know'd he was one o' the regular threepennies. Private room! and a lady too! If he's anything of a gen'l'm'n, he's vurth a shillin' a day, let alone the arrands.' Stimulated by this inspiring reflection, Mr Samuel brushed away with such hearty good-will, that in a few minutes the boots and shoes, with a polish which would have struck envy to the soul of the amiable Mr Warren (for they used Day & Martin at the White Hart), had arrived at the door of number five.

'Come in,' said a man's voice, in reply to Sam's rap at the door. Sam made his best bow, and stepped into the presence of a lady and gentleman seated at breakfast. Having officiously deposited the gentleman's boots right and left at his feet, and the lady's shoes right and left at hers, he backed towards the door.

'Boots,' said the gentleman.

'Sir,' said Sam, closing the door, and keeping his hand on the knob of the lock.

'Do you know – what's a-name – Doctors' Commons?'

'Yes, Sir.'

'Where is it?'

'Paul's Churchyard, Sir; low archway on the carriage side, bookseller's at one corner, hotel on the other, and two porters in the middle as touts for licences.'

'Touts for licences!' said the gentleman.

'Touts for licences,' replied Sam. 'Two coves in vhite aprons – touches their hats ven you walk in – "Licence, Sir, licence?" Queer sort, them, and their mas'rs, too, Sir – Old Bailey Proctors – and no mistake.'

'What do they do?' inquired the gentleman.

'Do! *You*, Sir! That ain't the worst on it, neither. They puts things into old gen'l'm'n's heads as they never dreamed of. My father, Sir, wos a coachman. A widower he wos, and fat enough for anything – uncommon fat, to be sure. His missus dies, and leaves him four hundred pound. Down he goes to the Commons, to see the lawyer and draw the blunt – very smart – top boots on – nosegay in his button-hole – broad-brimmed tile – green shawl – quite the gen'l'm'n. Goes through the archvay, thinking how he should inwest the money – up comes the touter, touches his hat – "Licence, Sir, licence?" – "What's that?" says my father. – "Licence, Sir," says he. – "What licence?" says my father. – "Marriage licence," says the touter. – "Dash my veskit," says my father, "I never thought o' that." – "I think you wants one, Sir," says the touter. My father pulls up, and thinks a bit – "No," says he, "damme, I'm too old, b'sides, I'm a many sizes too large," says he. – "Not a bit on it, Sir," says the touter. – "Think not?" says my father. – "I'm sure not," says he; "we married a gen'l'm'n twice your size, last Monday." – "Did you, though?" said my father. – "To be sure, we did," says the touter, "you're a babby to him – this way, sir – this way!" – and sure enough my father walks arter him, like a tame monkey behind a horgan, into a little back office, vere a teller sat among dirty papers, and tin boxes, making believe he was busy. "Pray take a seat, vile I makes out the affidavit, Sir," says the lawyer. – "Thank'ee, Sir," says my father, and down he sat, and stared with all his eyes, and his mouth vide open, at the names on the boxes. "What's your name, Sir," says the lawyer. – "Tony Weller," says my father. – "Parish?" says the lawyer. "Belle Savage," says my father; for he stopped there wen he drove up, and he know'd nothing about parishes, he didn't. – "And what's the lady's name?" says the lawyer. My father was struck all of a heap. "Blessed if I know," says he. – "Not know!" says the lawyer. – "No more nor you do," says my father; "can't I put that in arterwards?" – "Impossible!" says the lawyer. – "Wery well," says my father, after he'd thought a moment, "put down Mrs Clarke." – "What Clarke?" says the lawyer, dipping his pen in the ink. – "Susan Clarke, Markis o' Granby, Dorking," says my father; "she'll have me, if I ask. I des-say – I never said nothing to her, but she'll have me, I know." The licence was made out, and she *did* have him, and what's more she's got him now; and I never had any of the four hundred pound, worse luck. Beg your pardon, sir,' said Sam, when he had concluded, 'but wen I gets on this here grievance, I runs on like a new barrow with the wheel greased.' Having said which, and having paused for an instant to see whether he was wanted for anything more, Sam left the room.

From *The Posthumous Papers of the Pickwick Club*

Alternatively, a long walk from City Road to Thames Street, with Florence Dombey

WITH A WILD confusion before her, of people running up and down, and shouting, and wheels running over them, and boys fighting, and mad bulls coming up, and the nurse in the midst of all these dangers being torn to pieces, Florence screamed and ran. She ran till she was exhausted, urging Susan to do the same; and then, stopping and wringing her hands as she remembered they had left the other nurse behind, found, with a sensation of terror not to be described, that she was quite alone.

'Susan! Susan!' cried Florence, clapping her hands in the very ecstasy of her alarm. 'Oh, where are they? where are they?'

'Where are they?' said an old woman, coming hobbling across as fast as she could from the opposite side of the way. 'Why did you run away from 'em?'

'I was frightened,' answered Florence. 'I didn't know what I did. I thought they were with me. Where are they?'

The old woman took her by the wrist, and said, 'I'll show you.'

She was a very ugly old woman, with red rims round her eyes, and a mouth that mumbled and chattered of itself when she was not speaking. She was miserably dressed, and carried some skins over her arm. She seemed to have followed Florence some little way at all events, for she had lost her breath; and this made her uglier still, as she stood trying to regain it: working her shrivelled yellow face and throat into all sorts of contortions.

Florence was afraid of her, and looked, hesitating, up the street, of which she had almost reached the bottom. It was a solitary place – more a back road than a street – and there was no one in it but herself and the old woman.

'You needn't be frightened now,' said the old woman, still holding her tight. 'Come along with me.'

'I – I don't know you. What's your name?' asked Florence.

'Mrs Brown,' said the old woman. 'Good Mrs Brown.'

'Are they near here?' asked Florence, beginning to be led away.

'Susan ain't far off,' said Good Mrs Brown; 'and the others are close to her.'

'Is anybody hurt?' cried Florence.

'Not a bit of it,' said Good Mrs Brown.

The child shed tears of delight on hearing this, and accompanied the old woman willingly; though she could not help glancing at her face as they went along – particularly at that industrious mouth – and wondering whether Bad Mrs Brown, if there were such a person, was at all like her.

They had not gone far, but had gone by some very uncomfortable places, such as brick-fields and tile-yards, when the old woman turned down a dirty lane, where the mud lay in deep black ruts in the middle of the road. She stopped before a shabby little house, as closely shut up as a house that was full of cracks and crevices could be. Opening the door with a key she took out of her bonnet, she pushed the child before her into a back room, where there was a great heap of rags of different colours lying on the floor; a heap of bones, and a heap of sifted dust or cinders; but there was no furniture at all, and the walls and ceiling were quite black.

The child became so terrified the she was stricken speechless, and looked as though about to swoon.

'Now don't be a young mule,' said Good Mrs Brown, reviving her with a shake. 'I'm not a going to hurt you. Sit upon the rags.'

Florence obeyed her, holding out her folded hands, in mute supplication.

'I'm not a going to keep you, even, above an hour,' said Mrs Brown. 'D'ye understand what I say?'

The child answered with great difficulty, 'Yes.'

'Then,' said Good Mrs Brown, taking her own seat on the bones, 'don't vex me. If you don't, I tell you I won't hurt you. But if you do, I'll kill you. I could have you killed at any time – even if you was in your own bed at home. Now let's know who you are, and what you are, and all about it.'

The old woman's threats and promises; the dread of giving her offence; and the habit, unusual to a child, but almost natural to Florence now, of being quiet, and repressing what she felt, and feared, and hoped; enabled her to do this bidding, and to tell her little history, or what she knew of it. Mrs Brown listened attentively, until she had finished.

'So your name's Dombey, eh?' said Mrs Brown.

'I want that pretty frock, Miss Dombey,' said Good Mrs Brown, 'and that little bonnet, and a petticoat or two, and anything else you can spare. Come! Take 'em off.'

Florence obeyed, as fast as her trembling hands would allow; keeping, all the while, a frightened eye on Mrs Brown. When she had divested herself of all the articles of apparel mentioned by that lady, Mrs B. examined them at leisure, and seemed tolerably well satisfied with their quality and value.

'Humph!' she said, running her eyes over the

child's slight figure, 'I don't see anything else – except the shoes. I must have the shoes, Miss Dombey.'

Poor little Florence took them off with equal alacrity, only too glad to have any more means of conciliation about her. The old woman then produced some wretched substitutes from the bottom of the heap of rags, which she turned up for that purpose; together with a girl's cloak, quite worn out and very old; and the crushed remains of a bonnet that had probably been picked up from some ditch or dunghill. In this dainty raiment, she instructed Florence to dress herself; and as such preparation seemed a prelude to her release, the child complied with increased readiness, if possible.

In hurriedly putting on the bonnet, if that may be called a bonnet which was more like a pad to carry loads on, she caught it in her hair which grew luxuriantly, and could not immediately disentangle it. Good Mrs Brown whipped out a large pair of scissors, and fell into an unaccountable state of excitement.

'Why couldn't you let me be!' said Mrs Brown, 'when I was contented? You little fool!'

'I beg your pardon. I don't know what I have done,' panted Florence. 'I couldn't help it.'

'Couldn't help it!' cried Mrs Brown. 'How do you expect I can help it? Why, Lord!' said the old woman, ruffling her curls with a furious pleasure, 'anybody but me would have had 'em off, first of all.' Florence was so relieved to find that it was only her hair and not her head which Mrs Brown coveted, that she offered no resistance or entreaty, and merely raised her mild eyes towards the face of that good soul.

'If I hadn't once had a gal of my own – beyond seas now – that was proud of her hair,' said Mrs Brown, 'I'd have had every lock of it. She's far away, she's far away! Oho! Oho!'

Mrs Brown's was not a melodious cry, but, accompanied with a wild tossing up of her lean arms, it was full of passionate grief, and thrilled to the heart of Florence, whom it frightened more than ever. It had its part, perhaps, in saving her curls; for Mrs Brown, after hovering about her with the scissors for some moments, like a new kind of butterfly, bade her hide them under the bonnet and let no trace of them escape to tempt her. Having accomplished this victory over herself, Mrs Brown resumed her seat on the bones, and smoked a very short black pipe, mowing and mumbling all the time, as if she were eating the stem.

When the pipe was smoked out, she gave the child a rabbit-skin to carry, that she might appear the more like her ordinary companion, and told her that she was now going to lead her to a public street whence she could inquire her way to her friends. But she cautioned her, with threats of summary and deadly vengeance in case of disobedience, not to talk to strangers, nor to repair to her own home (which may have been too near for Mrs Brown's convenience), but to her father's office in the City; also to wait at the street corner where she would be left, until the clock struck three. These directions Mrs Brown enforced with assurances that there would be potent eyes and ears in her employment cognizant of all she did; and these directions Florence promised faithfully and earnestly to observe.

At length, Mrs Brown, issuing forth, conducted her changed and ragged little friend through a labyrinth of narrow streets and lanes and alleys, which emerged, after a long time, upon a stable yard, with a gateway at the end, whence the roar of a great thoroughfare made itself audible. Pointing out this gateway, and informing Florence that when the clocks struck three she was to go to the left, Mrs Brown, after making a parting grasp at her hair which seemed involuntary and quite beyond her own control, told her she knew what to do, and bade her go and do it: remembering that she was watched.

With a lighter heart, but still sore afraid, Florence felt herself released, and tripped off to the corner. When she reached it, she looked back and saw the head of Good Mrs Brown peeping out of the low wooden passage, where she had issued her parting injunctions; likewise the fist of Good Mrs Brown shaking towards her. But though she often looked back afterwards – every minute, at least, in her nervous recollection of the old woman – she could not see her again.

Florence remained there, looking at the bustle in the street, and more and more bewildered by it; and in the meanwhile the clocks appeared to have made up their minds never to strike three any more. At last the steeples rang out three o'clock; there was one close by, so she couldn't be mistaken; and – after often looking over her shoulder, and often going a little way, and as often coming back again, lest the all-powerful spies of Mrs Brown should take offence – she hurried off, as fast as she could in her slipshod shoes, holding the rabbit-skin tight in her hand.

All she knew of her father's offices was that they belonged to Dombey and Son, and that that was a great power belonging to the City. So she could only ask the way to Dombey and Son's in the City; and as she generally made inquiry of children – being afraid to ask grown people – she got very little satisfaction indeed. But by dint of asking her way to the City after a while, and dropping the rest of her inquiry for the present, she really did advance, by slow degrees, towards the heart of that great region which is governed by the terrible Lord Mayor.

Tired of walking, repulsed and pushed about, stunned by the noise and confusion, anxious for her brother and the nurses, terrified by what she had undergone, and the prospect of encountering her angry father in such an altered state; perplexed and frightened alike by what had passed, and what was passing, and what was yet before her; Florence went upon her weary way with tearful eyes, and once or twice could not help stopping to ease her bursting heart by crying bitterly. But few people noticed her at those times, in the garb she wore: or if they did, believed that she was tutored to excite compassion, and passed on. Florence, too, called to her aid all the firmness and self-reliance of a character that her sad experience had prematurely formed and tried: and keeping the end she had in view steadily before her, steadily pursued it.

It was full two hours later in the afternoon than when she had started on this strange adventure, when, escaping from the clash and clangour of a narrow street full of carts and waggons, she peeped into a kind of wharf or landing-place upon the river-side, where there were a great many packages, casks, and boxes, strewn about; a large pair of wooden scales; and a little wooden house on wheels, outside of which, looking at the neighbouring masts and boats, a stout man stood whistling, with his pen behind his ear, and his hands in his pockets, as if his day's work were nearly done.

'Now then!' said this man, happening to turn

round. 'We haven't got anything for you, little girl. Be off!'

'If you please, is this the City?' asked the trembling daughter of the Dombeys.

'Ah! It's the City. You know that well enough, I daresay. Be off! We haven't got anything for you.'

'I don't want anything, thank you,' was the timid answer. 'Except to know the way to Dombey and Son's.'

The man who had been strolling carelessly towards her, seemed surprised by this reply, and looking attentively in her face, rejoined:

'Why, what can you want with Dombey and Son's?'

'To know the way there, if you please.'

The man looked at her yet more curiously, and rubbed the back of his head so hard in his wonderment that he knocked his own hat off.

'Joe!' he called to another man – a labourer – as he picked it up and put it on again.

'Joe it is!' said Joe.

'Where's that young spark of Dombey's who's been watching the shipment of them goods?'

'Just gone, by t'other gate,' said Joe.

'Call him back a minute.'

Joe ran up an archway, bawling as he went, and very soon returned with a blithe-looking boy.

'You're Dombey's jockey, ain't you?' said the first man.

'I'm in Dombey's House, Mr Clark,' returned the boy.

'Look'ye here, then,' said Mr Clark.

Obedient to the indication of Mr Clark's hand, the boy approached towards Florence, wondering, as well he might, what he had to do with her. But she, who had heard what passed, and who, besides the relief of so suddenly considering herself safe at her journey's end, felt reassured beyond all measure by his lively youthful face and manner, ran eagerly up to him, leaving one of the slipshod shoes upon the ground and caught his hand in both of hers.

'I am lost, if you please!' said Florence.

'Lost!' cried the boy.

'Yes, I was lost this morning, a long way from here – and I have had my clothes taken away, since – and I am not dressed in my own now – and my name is Florence Dombey, my little brother's only sister – and, oh dear, dear, take care of me, if you please!' sobbed Florence, giving full vent to the childish feelings she had so long suppressed, and bursting into tears. At the same time her miserable bonnet falling off, her hair came tumbling down about her face: moving to speechless admiration and commiseration, young Walter, nephew of Solomon Gills, Ships' Instrument-maker in general.

Mr Clark stood rapt in amazement: observing under his breath, I never saw such a start on this wharf before. Walter picked up the shoe, and put it on the little foot as the Prince in the story might have fitted Cinderella's slipper on. He hung the rabbit-skin over his left arm; gave the right to Florence; and felt, not to say like Richard Whittington – that is a tame comparison – but like Saint George of England, with the dragon lying dead before him.

From *Dombey and Son*

A tour at night, with Charles Dickens himself

SOME YEARS AGO, a temporary inability to sleep, referable to a distressing impression, caused me to walk about the streets all night, for a series of several nights. The disorder might have taken a long time to conquer, if it had been faintly experimented on in bed; but, it was soon defeated by the brisk treatment of getting up directly after lying down, and going out, and coming home tired at sunrise.

In the course of those nights, I finished my education in a fair amateur experience of houselessness. My principal object being to get through the night, the pursuit of it brought me into sympathetic relations with people who have no other object every night in the year.

The month was March, and the weather damp, cloudy, and cold. The sun not rising before half-past five, the night perspective looked sufficiently long at half-past twelve: which was about my time for confronting it.

The restlessness of a great city, and the way in which it tumbles and tosses before it can get to sleep, formed one of the first entertainments offered to the contemplation of us houseless people. It lasted about two hours. We lost a great deal of companionship when the late public-houses turned their lamps out, and when the potmen thrust the last brawling drunkards into the street; but stray vehicles and stray people were left us, after that. If we were very lucky, a policeman's rattle sprang and a fray turned up; but, in general, surprisingly little of this diversion was provided. Except in the Haymarket, which is the worst kept part of London, and about Kent-street in the Borough, and along a portion of the line of the Old Kent-road, the peace was seldom violently broken. But, it was always the case that London, as if in imitation of individual citizens belonging to it, had expiring fits and starts of restlessness. After all seemed quiet, if one cab rattled by, half-a-dozen would surely follow; and Houselessness even observed that intoxicated people appeared to be magnetically attracted towards each other; so that we knew when we saw one drunken object staggering against the shutters of a shop, that another drunken object would stagger up before five minutes were out, to fraternise or fight with it. When we made a divergence from the regular species of drunkard, the thin-armed, puff-faced, leaden-lipped gin-drinker, and encountered a rarer specimen of a more decent appearance, fifty to one but that specimen was dressed in soiled mourning. As the street experience in the night, so the street experience in the day; the common folk who come unexpectedly into a little property, come unexpectedly into a deal of liquor.

At length these flickering sparks would die away, worn out – the last veritable sparks of waking life trailed from some late pieman or hot-potato man – and London would sink to rest. And then the yearning of the houseless mind would be for any sign of company, any lighted place, any movement, anything suggestive of any one being up – nay, even so much as awake, for the houseless eye looked out for lights in windows.

Walking the streets under the pattering rain, Houselessness would walk and walk and walk, seeing nothing but the interminable tangle of streets, save at a corner, here and there, two policemen in conversation, or the sergeant or inspector looking after his men. Now and then in the night – but rarely – Houselessness would become aware of a furtive head peering out of a doorway a few yards before him, and, coming up with the head, would find a man standing bolt upright to keep within the doorway's shadow, and evidently intent upon no particular service to society. Under a kind of fascination, and in a ghostly silence suitable to the time, Houselessness and this gentleman would eye one another from head to foot, and so, without exchange of speech, part, mutually suspicious. Drip, drip, drip, from ledge and coping, splash from pipes and waterspouts, and by-and-by the houseless shadow would fall upon the stones that pave the way to Waterloo-bridge; it being in the houseless mind to have a halfpenny worth of excuse for saying 'Good-night' to the toll-keeper, and catching a glimpse of his fire. A good fire and a good great-coat and a good woollen neck-shawl, were comfortable things to see in conjunction with the toll-keeper; also his brisk wakefulness was excellent company when he rattled the change of halfpence down upon that metal table of his, like a man who defied the night, with all its sorrowful thoughts, and didn't care for the coming of dawn. There was need of encouragement on the threshold of the bridge, for the bridge was dreary. The chopped-up murdered man, had not been lowered with a rope over the parapet when those nights were; he was alive, and slept then quietly enough most likely, and undisturbed by any dream of where he was to come. But the river had an awful look, the buildings on the banks were muffled in black shrouds, and the reflected lights seemed to originate deep in the water, as if the spectres of suicides were holding them to show where they went down. The wild moon and clouds were as restless as an evil conscience in a tumbled bed, and the very shadow of the immensity of London seemed to lie oppressively upon the river.

Between the bridge and the two great theatres, there was but the distance of a few hundred paces, so the theatres came next. Grim and black within, at night, those great dry wells, and lonesome to imagine, with the rows of faces faded out, the lights extinguished, and the seats all empty. One would think that nothing in them knew itself at such a time but Yorick's skull. In one of my night walks, as the church steeples were shaking the March winds and rain with the strokes of Four, I passed the outer boundary of one of these great deserts, and entered it. With a dim lantern in my hand, I groped my well-known way to the stage and looked over the orchestra – which was like a great grave dug for a time of pestilence – into the void beyond. A dismal cavern of an immense aspect, with the chandelier gone dead like everything else, and nothing visible through mist and fog and space, but tiers of winding-sheets. The ground at my feet where, when last there, I had seen the peasantry of Naples dancing among the vines, reckless of the burning mountain which threatened to overwhelm them, was now in possession of a strong serpent of engine-hose, watchfully lying in wait for the serpent Fire, and ready to fly at it if it showed its forked tongue. A ghost of a watchman, carrying a faint corpse candle, haunted the distant upper gallery and flitted away. Retiring within the proscenium, and holding my light above my head towards the rolled-up curtain – green no more, but black as ebony – my sight lost itself in a gloomy vault, showing faint indications in it of a shipwreck of canvas and cordage. Methought I felt much as a diver might, at the bottom of the sea.

In those small hours when there was no movement in the streets, it afforded matter for reflection to take Newgate in the way, and, touching its rough stone, to think of the prisoners in their sleep, and then to glance in at the lodge over the spiked wicket, and see the fire and light of the watching turnkeys, on the white wall. Not an inappropriate time either, to linger by that wicked little Debtors' Door – shutting tighter than any other door one ever saw – which has been Death's Door to so many. In the days of the uttering of forged one-pound notes by people tempted up from the country, how many hundreds of wretched creatures of both sexes – many quite innocent – swung out of a pitiless and inconsistent world, with the tower of yonder Christian church of Saint Sepulchre monstrously before their eyes! Is there any haunting of the Bank Parlour, by the remorseful souls of old directors, in the nights of these later days, I wonder, or is it as quiet as this degenerate Aceldama of an Old Bailey?

To walk on to the Bank, lamenting the good old times and bemoaning the present evil period, would be an easy next step, so I would take it, and would make my houseless circuit of the Bank, and give a thought to the treasure within; likewise to the guard of soldiers passing the night there, and nodding over the fire. Next, I went to Billingsgate, in some hope of market-people, but it proving as yet too early, crossed London-bridge and got down by the water-side on the Surrey shore among the buildings of the great brewery. There was plenty going on at the brewery; and the reek, and the smell of grains, and the rattling of the plump dray horses at their mangers, were capital company. Quite refreshed by having mingled with this good society, I made a new start with a new heart, setting the old King's Bench prison before me for my next object, and resolving, when I should come to the wall, to think of poor Horace Kinch, and the Dry Rot in men.

A very curious disease the Dry Rot in men, and difficult to detect the beginning of. It had carried Horace Kinch inside the wall of the old King's Bench prison, and it had carried him out with his feet foremost. He was a likely man to look at, in the prime of life, well to do, as clever as he needed to be, and popular among many friends. He was suitably married, and had healthy and pretty children. But, like some fair-looking houses or fair-looking ships, he took the Dry Rot. The first strong external revelation of the Dry Rot in men, is a tendency to lurk and lounge; to be at street-corners without intelligible reason; to be going anywhere when met; to be about many places rather than at any; to do nothing tangible, but to have an intention of performing a variety of intangible duties tomorrow or the day after. When this manifestation of the disease is observed, the observer will usually connect it with a vague impression once formed or received, that the patient was living a little too hard. He will scarcely have had leisure to turn it over in his mind and form the terrible suspicion 'Dry Rot,' when he will notice a change for the worse in the patient's appearance: a certain slovenliness and deterioration, which is not poverty, nor dirt, nor intoxication, nor ill-health, but simply Dry Rot. To this, succeeds a smell as of strong waters, in the morning; to that, a looseness respecting money; to that, a stronger smell as of strong waters, at all times; to that, a looseness respecting everything; to that, a trembling of the limbs, somnolency, misery, and crumbling to pieces. As it is in wood, so it is in men. Dry Rot advances at a compound usury quite incalculable. A plank is found infected with it, and the whole structure is devoted.

Thus it had been with the unhappy Horace Kinch, lately buried by a small subscription. Those who knew him had not nigh done saying, 'So well off, so comfortably established, with such hope before him – and yet, it is feared, with a slight touch of Dry Rot!' when lo! the man was all Dry Rot and dust.

From the dead wall associated on those houseless nights with this too common story, I chose next to wander by Bethlehem Hospital; partly, because it lay on my road round to Westminster; partly, because I had a night fancy in my head which could be best pursued within sight of its walls and dome. And the fancy was this: Are not the sane and the insane equal at night as the sane lie a dreaming? Are not all of us outside this hospital, who dream, more or less in the condition of those inside it, every night of our lives? Are we not nightly persuaded, as they daily are, that we associate preposterously with kings and queens, emperors and empresses, and notabilities of all sorts? Do we not nightly jumble events and personages and times and places, as these do daily? Are we not sometimes troubled by our own sleeping inconsistencies, and do we not vexedly try to account for them or excuse them, just as these do sometimes in respect of their waking delusions? Said an afflicted man to me, when I was last in a hospital like this, 'Sir, I can frequently fly.' I was half ashamed to reflect that so could I – by night. Said a woman to me on the same occasion, 'Queen Victoria frequently comes to dine with me, and her Majesty and I dine off peaches and maccaroni in our night-gowns, and his Royal Highness the Prince Consort does us the honour to make a third on horseback in a Field-Marshal's uniform.' Could I refrain from reddening with consciousness when I remembered the amazing royal parties I myself had given (at night), the unaccountable viands I had put on table, and my extraordinary manner of conducting myself on those distinguished occasions? I wonder that the great master who knew everything, when he called Sleep the death of each day's life, did not call Dreams the insanity of each day's sanity.

By this time I had left the Hospital behind me, and was again setting towards the river; and in a short breathing space I was on Westminster-bridge, regaling my houseless eyes with the external walls of the British Parliament – the perfection of a stupendous institution, I know, and the admiration of all surrounding nations and succeeding ages, I do not doubt, but perhaps a little the better now and then for being pricked up to its work. Turning off into Old Palace-yard, the Courts of Law kept me company for a quarter of an hour; hinting in low whispers what numbers of people they were keeping awake, and how intensely wretched and horrible they were rendering the small hours to unfortunate suitors.

Westminster Abbey was fine gloomy society for another quarter of an hour; suggesting a wonderful procession of its dead among the dark arches and pillars, each century more amazed by the century following it than by all the centuries going before. And indeed in those houseless night walks – which even included cemeteries where watchmen went round among the graves at stated times, and moved the tell-tale handle of an index which recorded that they had touched it at such an hour – it was a solemn consideration what enormous hosts of dead belong to one old great city, and how, if they were raised while the living slept, there would not be the space of a pin's point in all the streets and ways for the living to come out into. Not only that, but the vast armies of dead would overflow the hills and valleys beyond the city, and would stretch away all round it, God knows how far.

When a church clock strikes, on houseless ears in the dead of the night, it may be at first mistaken for company and hailed as such. But, as the spreading circles of vibration, which you may perceive at such a time with great clearness, go opening out, for ever and ever afterwards widening perhaps (as the philosopher has suggested) in eternal space, the mistake is rectified and the sense of loneliness is profounder. Once – it was after leaving the Abbey and turning my face north – I came to the great steps of St Martin's church as the clock was striking Three. Suddenly, a thing that in a moment more I should have trodden upon without seeing, rose up at my feet with a cry of loneliness and houselessness, struck out of it by the bell, the like of which I never heard. We then stood face to face looking at one another, frightened by one another. The creature was like a beetle-browed hair-lipped youth of twenty, and it had a loose bundle of rags on, which it held together with one of its hands. It shivered from head to foot, and its teeth chattered, and as it stared at me – persecutor, devil, ghost, whatever it thought me – it made with its whining mouth as if it were snapping at me, like a worried dog. Intending to give this ugly object money, I put out my hand to stay it – for it recoiled as it whined and snapped – and laid my hand upon its shoulder. Instantly, it twisted out of its garment, like the young man in the New Testament, and left me standing alone with its rags in my hands.

Covent-garden Market, when it was market morning, was wonderful company. The great waggons of cabbages, with growers' men and boys lying asleep under them, and with sharp dogs from market-garden neighbourhoods looking after the whole, were as good as a party. But one of the worst night sights I know in London, is to be found in the children who prowl about this place; who sleep in the baskets, fight for the offal, dart at any object they think they can lay their thieving hands on, dive under the carts and barrows, dodge the constables, and are perpetually making a blunt pattering on the pavement of the Piazza with the rain of their naked feet. A painful and unnatural result comes of the comparison one is forced to institute between the growth of corruption as displayed in the so much improved and cared for fruits of the earth, and the growth of corruption as displayed in these all uncared for (except inasmuch as ever-hunted) savages.

There was early coffee to be got about Covent-garden Market, and that was more company – warm company, too, which was better. Toast of a very substantial quality, was likewise procurable: though the towzled-headed man who made it, in an inner chamber within the coffee-room, hadn't got his coat on yet, and was so heavy with sleep that in every interval of toast and coffee he went off anew behind the partition into complicated cross-roads of choke and snore, and lost his way directly. Into one of these establishments (among the earliest) near Bow-street, there came one morning as I sat over my houseless cup, pondering where to go next, a man in a high and long snuff-coloured coat, and shoes, and, to the best of my belief, nothing else but a hat, who took out of his hat a large cold meat pudding; a meat pudding so large that it was a very tight fit, and brought the lining of the hat out with it. This mysterious man was known by his pudding, for on his entering, the man of sleep brought him a pint of hot tea, a small loaf, and a large knife and fork and plate. Left to himself in his box, he stood the pudding on the bare table, and, instead of cutting it, stabbed it, overhand, with the knife, like a mortal enemy; then took the knife out, wiped it on his sleeve, tore the pudding asunder with his fingers, and ate it all up. The remembrance of this man with the pudding remains with me as the remembrance of the most spectral person my houselessness encountered. Twice only was I in that establishment, and twice I saw him stalk in (as I should say, just out of bed, and presently going back to bed), take out his pudding, stab his pudding, wipe the dagger, and eat his pudding all up. He was a man whose figure promised cadaverousness, but who had an excessively red face, though shaped like a horse's. On the second occasion of my seeing him, he said huskily to the man of sleep, 'Am I red to-night?' 'You are,' he uncompromisingly answered. 'My mother,' said the spectre, 'was a red-faced woman that liked drink, and I looked at her hard when she laid in her coffin, and I took the complexion.' Somehow, the pudding seemed an unwholesome pudding after that, and I put myself in its way no more.

When there was no market, or when I wanted variety, a railway terminus with the morning mails coming in, was remunerative company. But like most of the company to be had in this world, it lasted only a very short time. The station lamps would burst out ablaze, the porters would emerge from places of concealment, the cabs and trucks would rattle to their places (the post-office carts were already in theirs), and, finally, the bell would strike up, and the train would come banging in. But there were few passengers and little luggage, and everything scuttled away with the greatest expedition. The locomotive post-offices, with their great nets – as if they had been dragging the country for bodies – would fly open as to their doors, and would disgorge a smell of lamp, an exhausted clerk, a guard in a red coat, and their bags of letters; the engine would blow and heave and perspire, like an engine wiping its forehead and saying what a run it had had; and within ten minutes the lamps were out, and I was houseless and alone again.

But now, there were driven cattle on the high road near, wanting (as cattle always do) to turn into the midst of stone walls, and squeeze themselves through six inches' width of iron railing, and getting their heads down (also as cattle always do) for tossing-purchase at quite imaginary dogs, and giving themselves and every devoted creature associated with them a most extraordinary amount of unnecessary trouble. Now, too, the conscious gas began to grow pale with the knowledge that daylight was coming, and straggling workpeople were already in the streets, and, as waking life had become extinguished with the last pieman's sparks, so it began to be rekindled with the fires of the first street-corner breakfast-sellers. And so by faster and faster degrees, until the last degrees were very fast, the day came, and I was tired and could sleep. And it is not, as I used to think, going home at such times, the least wonderful thing in London, that in the real desert region of the night, the houseless wanderer is alone there. I knew well enough where to find Vice and Misfortune of all kinds, if I had chosen; but they were put out of sight, and my houselessness had many miles upon miles of streets in which it could, and did, have its own solitary way.

From *The Uncommercial Traveller*

Another night tour, out of the city from Bethnal Green and . . . Back again, with Bill Sykes

OF ALL BAD deeds that, under cover of the darkness, had been committed within wide London's bounds since night hung over it, that was the worst. Of all the horrors that rose with an ill scent upon the morning air, that was the foulest and most cruel.

The sun – the bright sun, that brings back, not light alone, but new life, and hope, and freshness to man – burst upon the crowded city in clear and radiant glory. Through costly-coloured glass and paper-mended window, through cathedral dome and rotten crevice, it shed its equal ray. It lighted up the room where the murdered woman lay. It did. He tried to shut it out, but it would stream in. If the sight had been a ghastly one in the dull morning, what was it, now, in all that brilliant light!

He had not moved; he had been afraid to stir.

There had been a moan and motion of the hand; and, with terror added to rage, he had struck and struck again. Once he threw a rug over it; but it was worse to fancy the eyes, and imagine them moving towards him, than to see them glaring upward, as if watching the reflection of the pool of gore that quivered and danced in the sunlight on the ceiling. He had plucked it off again. And there was the body – mere flesh and blood, no more – but such flesh, and so much blood!

He struck a light, kindled a fire, and thrust the club into it. There was hair upon the end, which blazed and shrunk into a light cinder, and, caught by the air, whirled up the chimney. Even that frightened him, sturdy as he was; but he held the weapon till it broke, and then piled it on the coals to burn away, and smoulder into ashes. He washed himself, and rubbed his clothes; there were spots that would not be removed, but he cut the pieces out, and burnt them. How those stains were dispersed about the room! The very feet of the dog were bloody.

All this time he had, never once, turned his back upon the corpse; no, not for a moment. Such preparations completed, he moved, backward, towards the door: dragging the dog with him, lest he should soil his feet anew and carry out new evidence of the crime into the streets. He shut the door softly, locked it, took the key, and left the house.

He crossed over, and glanced up at the window, to

be sure that nothing was visible from the outside. There was the curtain still drawn, which she would have opened to admit the light she never saw again. It lay nearly under there. *He* knew that. God, how the sun poured down upon the very spot!

The glance was instantaneous. It was a relief to have got free of the room. He whistled on the dog, and walked rapidly away.

He went through Islington; strode up the hill at Highgate on which stands the stone in honour of Whittington; turned down to Highgate Hill, unsteady of purpose, and uncertain where to go; struck off to the right again, almost as soon as he began to descend it; and taking the foot-path across the fields, skirted Caen Wood, and so came on Hampstead Heath. Traversing the hollow by the Vale of Heath, he mounted the opposite bank, and crossing the road which joins the villages of Hampstead and Highgate, made along the remaining portion of the heath to the fields at North End, in one of which he laid himself down under a hedge, and slept.

Soon he was up again, and away, – not far into the country, but back towards London by the high-road – then back again – then over another part of the same ground as he already traversed – then wandering up and down in fields, and lying on ditches' brinks to rest, and starting up to make for some other spot, and do the same, and ramble on again.

Where could he go, that was near and not too public, to get some meat and drink? Hendon. That was a good place, not far off, and out of most people's way. Thither he directed his steps, – running sometimes, and sometimes, with a strange perversity, loitering at a snail's pace, or stopping altogether and idly breaking the hedges with a stick. But when he got there, all the people he met – the very children at the doors – seemed to view him with suspicion. Back he turned again, without the courage to purchase bit or drop, though he had tasted no food for many hours; and once more he lingered on the Heath, uncertain where to go.

He wandered over miles and miles of ground, and still came back to the old place. Morning and noon had passed, and the day was on the wane, and still he rambled to and fro, and up and down, and round and round, and still lingered about the same spot. At last he got away, and shaped his course for Hatfield.

It was nine o'clock at night, when the man, quite tired out, and the dog, limping and lame from the unaccustomed exercise, turned down the hill by the church of the quiet village, and plodding along the little street, crept into a small public-house, whose scanty light had guided them to the spot. There was a fire in the tap-room, and some country-labourers were drinking before it.

They made room for the stranger, but he sat down

in the furthest corner, and ate and drank alone, or rather with his dog: to whom he cast a morsel of food from time to time.

The conversation of the men assembled here, turned upon the neighbouring land, and farmers; and when those topics were exhausted, upon the age of some old man who had been buried on the previous Sunday; the young men present considering him very old, and the old men present declaring him to have been quite young – not older, one white-haired grandfather said, than he was – with ten or fifteen year of life in him at least – if he had taken care; if he had taken care.

There was nothing to attract attention, or excite alarm in this. The robber, after paying his reckoning, sat silent and unnoticed in his corner, and had almost dropped asleep, when he was half wakened by the noisy entrance of a new comer.

This was an antic fellow, half pedlar and half mountebank, who travelled about the country on foot to vend hones, strops, razors, washballs, harness-paste, medicine for dogs and horses, cheap perfumery, cosmetics, and such-like wares, which he carried in a case slung to his back. His entrance was the signal for various homely jokes with the countrymen, which slackened not until he had made his supper, and opened his box of treasures, when he ingeniously contrived to unite business with amusement.

'And what be that stoof? Good to eat, Harry?' asked a grinning countryman, pointing to some composition-cakes in one corner.

'This,' said the fellow, producing one, 'this is the infallible and invaluable composition for removing all sorts of stain, rust, dirt, mildew, spick, speck, spot, or spatter, from silk, satin, linen, cambric, cloth, crape, stuff, carpet, merino, muslin, bombazeen, or woollen stuff. Wine-stains, fruit-stains, beer-stains, water-stains, paint-stains, pitch-stains, any stains, all come out at one rub with the infallible and invaluablc composition. If a lady stains her honour, she has only need to swallow one cake and she's cured at once – for it's poison. If a gentleman wants to prove this, he has only need to bolt one little square, and he has put it beyond question – for it's quite as satisfactory as a pistol-bullet, and a great deal nastier in the flavour, consequently the more credit in taking it. One penny a square. With all these virtues, one penny a square!'

There were two buyers directly, and more of the listeners plainly hesitated. The vendor observing this, increased in loquacity.

'It's all bought up as fast as it can be made,' said the fellow. 'There are fourteen water-mills, six steam-engines, and a galvanic battery, always a-working upon it, and they can't make it fast enough, though the men work so hard that they die off, and the widows is pensioned directly, with twenty pound a-year for each of the children, and a premium of fifty for twins. One penny a square! Two half-pence is all the same, and four farthings is received with joy. One penny a square! Wine-stains, fruit-stains, beer-stains, water-stains, paint-stains, pitch-stains, mud-stains, blood-stains! Here is a stain upon the hat of a gentleman in company, that I'll take clean out, before he can order me a pint of ale.'

'Hah!' cried Sikes starting up. 'Give that back.'

'I'll take it clean out, sir,' replied the man, winking to the company, 'before you can come across the room to get it. Gentlemen all, observe the dark stain upon this gentleman's hat, no wider than a shilling, but thicker than a half-crown. Whether it is a wine-stain, fruit-stain, beer-stain, water-stain, paint-stain, pitch-stain, mud-stain, or blood-stain –'

The man got no further, for Sikes with a hideous imprecation overthrew the table, and tearing the hat from him, burst out of the house.

With the same perversity of feeling and irresolution that had fastened upon him, despite himself, all day, the murderer, finding that he was not followed, and that they most probably considered him some drunken sullen fellow, turned back up the town, and getting out of the glare of the lamps of a stage-coach that was standing in the street, was walking past, when he recognised the mail from London, and saw that it was standing at the little post-office. He almost knew what was to come; but he crossed over, and listened.

The guard was standing at the door, waiting for the letter-bag. A man, dressed like a game-keeper, came up at the moment, and he handed him a basket which lay ready on the pavement.

'That's for your people,' said the guard. 'Now, look alive in there, will you. Damn that 'ere bag, it warn't ready night afore last; this won't do, you know!'

'Anything new up in town, Ben?' asked the game-keeper, drawing back to the window-shutters, the better to admire the horses.

'No, nothing that I knows on,' replied the man, pulling on his gloves. 'Corn's up a little. I heerd talk of a murder, too, down Spitalfields way, but I don't reckon much upon it.'

'Oh, that's quite true,' said a gentleman inside, who was looking out of the window. 'And a dreadful murder it was.'

'Was it, sir?' rejoined the guard, touching his hat. 'Man or woman, pray, sir?'

'A woman,' replied the gentleman. 'It is supposed –'

'Now, Ben,' replied the coachman impatiently.

'Damn that 'ere bag,' said the guard; 'are you gone to sleep in there?'

'Coming!' cried the office keeper, running out.

'Coming,' growled the guard. 'Ah, and so's the young 'ooman of property that's going to take a fancy to me, but I don't know when. Here, give hold. All ri-ight!'

The horn sounded a few cheerful notes, and the coach was gone.

Sikes remained standing in the street, apparently unmoved by what he had just heard, and agitated by no stronger feeling than a doubt where to go. At length he went back again, and took the road which leads from Hatfield to St Albans.

He went on doggedly; but as he left the town behind him, and plunged into the solitude and darkness of the road, he felt a dread and awe creeping upon him which shook him to the core. Every object before him, substance or shadow, still or moving, took the semblance of some fearful thing; but these fears were nothing compared to the sense that haunted him of that morning's ghastly figure following at his heels. He could trace its shadow in the gloom, supply the smallest item of the outline, and note how stiff and solemn it seemed to stalk along. He could hear its garments rustling in the leaves, and every breath of wind came laden with that last low cry. If he stopped it did the same. If he ran, it followed – not running too: that would have been a relief: but like a corpse endowed with the mere machinery of life, and borne on one slow melancholy wind that never rose or fell.

At times, he turned, with desperate determination,

resolved to beat this phantom off, though it should look him dead; but the hair rose on his head, and his blood stood still, for it had turned with him and was behind him then. He had kept it before him that morning, but it was behind now – always. He leaned his back against a bank, and felt that it stood above him, visibly out against the cold night-sky. He threw himself upon the road – on his back upon the road. At his head it stood, silent, erect, and still – a living grave-stone, with its epitaph in blood.

Let no man talk of murderers escaping justice, and hint that Providence must sleep. There were twenty score of violent deaths in one long minute of that agony of fear.

There was a shed in a field he passed, that offered shelter for the night. Before the door, were three tall poplar trees, which made it very dark within; and the wind moaned through them with a dismal wail. He *could not* walk on, till daylight came again; and here he stretched himself close to the wall – to undergo new torture.

For now, a vision came before him, as constant and more terrible than that from which he had escaped. Those widely staring eyes, so lustreless and so glassy, that he had better borne to see them than think upon them, appeared in the midst of the darkness: light in themselves, but giving light to nothing. There were but two, but they were everywhere. If he shut out the sight, there came the room with every well-known object – some, indeed, that he would have forgotten, if he had gone over its contents from memory – each in its accustomed place. The body was in *its* place, and its eyes were as he saw them when he stole away. He got up, and rushed into the field without. The figure was behind him. He re-entered the shed, and shrunk down once more. The eyes were there, before he had laid himself along.

And here he remained in such terror as none but he can know, trembling in every limb, and the cold sweat starting from every pore, when suddenly there arose upon the night-wind the noise of distant shouting, and the roar of voices mingled in alarm and wonder. Any sound of men in that lonely place, even though it conveyed a real cause of alarm, was something to him. He regained his strength and energy at the prospect of personal danger; and springing to his feet, rushed into the open air.

The broad sky seemed on fire. Rising into the air with showers of sparks, and rolling one above the other, were sheets of flame, lighting the atmosphere for miles round, and driving clouds of smoke in the direction where he stood. The shouts grew louder as new voices swelled the roar, and he could hear the cry of Fire! mingled with the ringing of an alarm-bell, the fall of heavy bodies, and the crackling of flames as they twined round some new obstacle, and shot aloft as though refreshed by food. The noise increased as he looked. There were people there – men and women – light, bustle. It was like new life to him. He darted onward – straight, headlong – dashing through brier and brake, and leaping gate and fence as madly as his dog, who careered with loud and sounding bark before him.

He came upon the spot. There were half-dressed figures tearing to and fro, some endeavouring to drag the frightened horses from the stables, others driving the cattle from the yard and out-houses, and others coming laden from the burning pile, amidst a shower of falling sparks, and the tumbling down of red-hot beams. The apertures, where doors and windows stood an hour ago, disclosed a mass of raging fire; walls rocked and crumbled into the burning well; the molten lead and iron poured down, white hot, upon the ground. Women and children shrieked, and men encouraged each other with noisy shouts and cheers. The clanking of the engine-pumps, and the spirting and hissing of the water as it fell upon the blazing wood, added to the tremendous roar. He shouted, too, till he was hoarse; and flying from memory and himself, plunged into the thickest of the throng. Hither and thither he dived that night: now working at the pumps, and now hurrying through the smoke and flame, but never ceasing to engage himself wherever noise and men were thickest. Up and down the ladders, upon the roofs of buildings, over floors that quaked and trembled with his weight, under the lee of falling bricks and stones, in every part of that great fire was he; but he bore a charmed life, and had neither scratch nor bruise, nor weariness nor thought, till morning dawned again, and only smoke and blackened ruins remained.

This mad excitement over, there returned, with ten-fold force, the dreadful consciousness of his crime. He looked suspiciously about him, for the men were conversing in groups, and he feared to be the subject of their talk. The dog obeyed the significant beck of his finger, and they drew off, stealthily, together. He passed near an engine where some men were seated, and they called to him to share in their refreshment. He took some bread and meat; and as he drank a draught of beer, heard the firemen, who were from London, talking about the murder. 'He has gone to Birmingham, they say,' said one: 'but they'll have him yet, for the scouts are out, and by to-morrow night there'll be a cry all through the country.'

He hurried off, and walked till he almost dropped upon the ground; then lay down in a lane, and had a long, but broken and uneasy sleep. He wandered on again, irresolute and undecided, and oppressed with the fear of another solitary night.

Suddenly, he took the desperate resolution to going back to London.

'There's somebody to speak to there, at all event,' he thought. 'A good hiding-place, too. They'll never expect to nab me there, after this country scent. Why can't I lie by for a week or so, and, forcing blunt from Fagin, get abroad to France? Damme, I'll risk it.'

He acted upon this impulse without delay, and choosing the least frequented roads began his journey back.

From *Oliver Twist*

After a dark night, a London morning

The appearance presented by the streets of London an hour before sunrise, on a summer's morning, is most striking even to the few whose unfortunate pursuits of pleasure, or scarcely less unfortunate pursuits of business, cause them to be well acquainted with the scene. There is an air of cold, solitary desolation about the noiseless streets which we are accustomed to see thronged at other times by a busy, eager crowd, and over the quiet, closely-shut buildings, which throughout the day are swarming with life and bustle, that is very impressive.

The last drunken man, who shall find his way home before sunlight, has just staggered heavily along, roaring out the burden of the drinking song of the previous night: the last houseless vagrant whom penury and police have left in the streets, has coiled up his chilly limbs in some paved corner, to dream of food and warmth. The drunken, the dissipated, and the wretched have disappeared; the more sober and orderly part of the population have not yet awakened to the labours of the day, and the stillness of death is over the streets; its very hue seems to be imparted to them, cold and lifeless as they look in the grey, sombre light of daybreak. The coach-stands in the larger thoroughfares are deserted: the night-houses are closed; and the chosen promenades of profligate misery are empty.

An occasional policeman may alone be seen at the street corners, listlessly gazing on the deserted prospect before him; and now and then a rakish-looking cat runs stealthily across the road and descends his own area with as much caution and slyness – bounding first on the water-butt, then on the dust-hole, and then alighting on the flag-stones – as if he were conscious that his character depended on his gallantry of the preceding night escaping public observation. A partially opened bedroom-window here and there, bespeaks the heat of the weather, and the uneasy slumbers of its occupant; and the dim scanty flicker of the rushlight, through the window-blind, denotes the chamber of watching or sickness. With these few exceptions, the streets present no signs of life, nor the houses of habitation.

An hour wears away; the spires of the churches and roofs of the principal buildings are faintly tinged with the light of the rising sun; and the streets, by almost imperceptible degrees, begin to resume their bustle and animation. Market-carts roll slowly along: the sleepy waggoner impatiently urging on his tired horses, or vainly endeavouring to awaken the boy, who, luxuriously stretched on the top of the fruit-baskets, forgets, in happy oblivion, his long-cherished curiosity to behold the wonders of London.

Rough, sleepy-looking animals of strange appearance, something between ostlers and hackney-coachmen, begin to take down the shutters of early public-houses; and little deal tables, with the ordinary preparations for a street breakfast, make their appearance at the customary stations. Numbers of men and women (principally the latter), carrying upon their heads heavy baskets of fruit, toil down the park side of Piccadilly, on their way to Covent-garden, and, following each other in rapid succession, form a long straggling line from thence to the turn of the road at Knightsbridge.

Here and there, a bricklayer's labourer, with the day's dinner tied up in a handkerchief, walks briskly to his work, and occasionally a little knot of three or four schoolboys on a stolen bathing expedition rattle merrily over the pavement, their boisterous mirth contrasting forcibly with the demeanour of the little sweep, who, having knocked and rung till his arm aches, and being interdicted by a merciful legislature from endangering his lungs by calling out, sits patiently down on the door-step, until the housemaid may happen to awake.

Covent-garden market, and the avenues leading to it, are thronged with carts of all sorts, sizes, and descriptions, from the heavy lumbering waggon, with its four stout horses, to the jingling costermonger's cart, with its consumptive donkey. The pavement is already strewed with decayed cabbage-leaves, broken hay-bands, and all the indescribable litter of a vegetable market; men are shouting, carts backing, horses neighing, boys fighting, basket-women talking, piemen expatiating on the excellence of their pastry, and donkeys braying. These and a hundred other sounds form a compound discordant enough to a Londoner's ears, and remarkably disagreeable to those of country gentlemen who are sleeping at the Hummums for the first time.

Another hour passes away, and the day begins in good earnest. The servant of all work, who, under the plea of sleeping very soundly, has utterly disregarded 'Missis's' ringing for half an hour previously, is warned by Master (whom Missis has sent up in his drapery to the landing-place for that purpose), that it's half-past six, whereupon she awakes all of a sudden, with well-feigned astonishment, and goes down-stairs very sulkily, wishing, while she strikes a light, that the principle of spontaneous combustion would extend itself to coals and kitchen range. When the fire is lighted, she opens the street-door to take in the milk, when, by the most singular coincidence in the world, she discovers that the servant next door has just taken in her milk too, and that Mr Todd's young man over the way, is, by an equally extraordinary chance, taking down his master's shutters. The inevitable consequence is, that she just steps, milk-jug in hand, as far as next door, just to say 'good morning' to Betsy Clark, and that Mr Todd's young man just steps over the way to say 'good morning' to both of 'em; and as the aforesaid Mr Todd's young man is almost as good-looking and fascinating as the baker himself, the conversation quickly becomes very interesting, and probably would become more so, if Betsy Clark's Missis, who always will be a-followin' her about, didn't give an angry tap at her bedroom window, on which Mr Todd's young man tries to whistle coolly, as he goes back to his shop much faster than he came from it; and the two girls run back to their respective places, and shut their street-doors with surprising softness, each of them poking their heads out of the front parlour window, a minute afterwards, however, ostensibly with the view of looking at the mail which just then passes by, but really for the purpose of catching another glimpse of Mr Todd's young man, who being fond of mails, but more of females, takes a short look at the mails, and a long look at the girls, much to the satisfaction of all parties concerned.

The mail itself goes on to the coach-office in due course, and the passengers who are going out by the early coach, stare with astonishment at the passengers who are coming in by the early coach, who look blue and dismal, and are evidently under the influence of that odd feeling produced by travelling, which makes the events of yesterday morning seem as if they had happened at least six months ago, and induces people to wonder with considerable gravity whether the friends and relations they took leave of a fortnight before, have altered much since they have left them. The coach-office is all alive, and the coaches which are just going out, are surrounded by the usual crowd of Jews and nondescripts, who seem to consider, Heaven knows why, that it is quite impossible any man can mount a coach without requiring at least sixpenny-worth of oranges, a penknife, a pocket-book, a last year's annual, a pencil-case, a piece of sponge, and a small series of caricatures.

Half an hour more, and the sun darts his bright rays cheerfully down the still half-empty streets, and shines with sufficient force to rouse the dismal laziness of the apprentice, who pauses every other minute from his task of sweeping out the shop and watering the pavement in front of it, to tell another apprentice similarly employed, how hot it will be to-day, or to stand with his right hand shading his eyes, and his left resting on the broom, gazing at the 'Wonder,' or the 'Tally-ho,' or the 'Nimrod,' or some other fast coach, till it is out of sight, when he re-enters the shop, envying the passengers on the outside of the fast coach, and thinking of the old red brick house 'down in the country,' where he went to school: the miseries of the milk and water, and thick bread and scrapings, fading into nothing before the pleasant recollection of the green field the boys used to play in, and the green pond he was caned for presuming to fall into, and other schoolboy associations.

Cabs, with trunks and band-boxes between the drivers' legs and outside the apron, rattle briskly up and down the streets on their way to the coach-offices or steam-packet wharfs; and the cab-drivers and hackney-coachmen who are on the stand polish up the ornamental part of their dingy vehicles – the former wondering how people can prefer 'them wild beast cariwans of homnibuses, to a riglar cab with a fast trotter,' and the latter admiring how people can trust their necks into one of 'them crazy cabs, when they can have a 'spectable 'ackney cotche with a pair of 'orses as von't run away with no vun;' a consolation unquestionably founded on fact, seeing that a hackney-coach horse never was known to run at all, 'except,' as the smart cabman in front of the rank observes, 'except one, and *he* run back'ards.'

The shops are now completely opened, and apprentices and shopmen are busily engaged in cleaning and decking the windows for the day. The bakers' shops in town are filled with servants and children waiting for the drawing of the first batch of rolls – an operation which was performed a full hour ago in the suburbs: for the early clerk population of Somers and Camden towns, Islington, and Pentonville, are fast pouring into the city, or directing their steps towards Chancery-lane and the Inns of Court. Middle-aged men, whose salaries have by no means increased in the same proportion as their families, plod steadily along, apparently with no object in view but the counting-house; knowing by sight almost everybody they meet or overtake, for they have seen them every morning (Sunday excepted) during the last twenty years, but speaking to no one. If they do happen to overtake a personal acquaintance, they just exchange a hurried salutation, and keep walking on either by his side, or in front of him, as his rate of walking may chance to be. As to stopping to shake hands, or to take the friend's arm, they seem to think that as it is not included in their salary, they have no right to do it. Small office lads in large hats, who are made men before they are boys, hurry along in pairs, with their first coat carefully brushed, and the white trousers of last Sunday plentifully besmeared with dust and ink. It evidently requires a considerable mental struggle to avoid investing part of the day's dinner-money in the purchase of the stale tarts so temptingly exposed in dusty tins at the pastry-cooks' doors; but a consciousness of their own importance and the receipt of seven shillings a-week, with the prospect of an early rise to eight, comes to their aid, and they accordingly put their hats a little more on one side, and look under the bonnets of all the milliners' and stay-makers' apprentices they meet – poor girls! – the hardest worked, the worst paid, and too often, the worst used class of the community.

Eleven o'clock, and a new set of people fill the streets. The goods in the shop-windows are invitingly arranged; the shopmen in their white neckerchiefs and spruce coats, look as it they couldn't clean a window if their lives depended on it; the carts have disappeared from Covent-garden; the waggoners have returned, and the costermongers repaired to their ordinary 'beats' in the suburbs; clerks are at their offices, and gigs, cabs, omnibuses, and saddle-horses, are conveying their masters to the same destination. The streets are thronged with a vast concourse of people, gay and shabby, rich and poor, idle and industrious; and we come to the heat, bustle, and activity of Noon.

From *Sketches by Boz*

Another morning, at Christmastime

THEY STOOD IN the city streets on Christmas morning, where (for the weather was severe) the people made a rough, but brisk and not unpleasant kind of music, in scraping the snow from the pavement in front of their dwellings, and from the tops of their houses, whence it was mad delight to the boys to see it come plumping down into the road below, and splitting into artificial little snow-storms.

The house fronts looked black enough, and the windows blacker, contrasting with the smooth white sheet of snow upon the roofs, and with the dirtier snow upon the ground; which last deposit had been ploughed up in deep furrows by the heavy wheels of carts and waggons; furrows that crossed and recrossed each other hundreds of times where the great streets branched off; and made intricate channels, hard to trace in the thick yellow mud and icy water. The sky was gloomy, and the shortest streets were choked up with a dingy mist, half thawed, half frozen, whose heavier particles descended in a shower of sooty atoms, as if all the chimneys in Great Britain had, by one consent, caught fire, and were blazing away to their dear hearts' content. There was nothing very cheerful in the climate or the town, and yet was there an air of cheerfulness abroad that the clearest summer air and brightest summer sun might have endeavoured to diffuse in vain.

For the people who were shovelling away on the housetops were jovial and full of glee; calling out to one another from the parapets, and now and then exchanging a facetious snowball – better-natured missile far than many a wordy jest – laughing heartily if it went right and not less heartily if it went wrong. The poulterers' shops were still half open, and the fruiterers' were radiant in their glory. There were great, round, pot-bellied baskets of chestnuts, shaped like the waistcoats of jolly old gentlemen, lolling at the doors, and tumbling out into the street in their apoplectic opulence. There were ruddy, brown-faced, broad-girthed Spanish onions, shining in the fatness of their growth like Spanish Friars, and winking from their shelves in wanton slyness at the girls as they went by, and glanced demurely at the hung-up mistletoe. There were pears and apples, clustered high in blooming pyramids; there were bunches of grapes, made, in the shopkeepers' benevolence, to dangle from conspicuous hooks, that people's mouths might water gratis as they passed; there were piles of filberts, mossy and brown, recalling, in their fragrance, ancient walks among the woods, and pleasant shufflings ankle deep through withered leaves; there were Norfolk Biffins, squat and swarthy, setting off the yellow of the oranges and lemons, and, in the great compactness of their juicy persons, urgently entreating and beseeching to be carried home in paper bags and eaten after dinner. The very gold and silver fish, set forth among these choice fruits in a bowl, though members of a dull and stagnant-blooded race, appeared to know that there was something going on; and, to a fish, went gasping round and round their little world in slow and passionless excitement.

The Grocers'! oh, the Grocers'! nearly closed, with perhaps two shutters down, or one; but through those gaps such glimpses! It was not alone that the scales descending on the counter made a merry sound, or that the twine and roller parted company so briskly, or that the canisters were rattled up and down like juggling tricks, or even that the blended scents of tea and coffee were so grateful to the nose, or even that the raisins were so plentiful and rare, the almonds so extremely white, the sticks of cinnamon so long and straight, the other spices so delicious, the candied fruits so caked and spotted with molten sugar as to make the coldest lookers-on feel faint and subsequently bilious. Nor was it that the figs were moist and pulpy, or that the French plums blushed in modest tartness from their highly-decorated boxes, or that everything was good to eat and in its Christmas dress; but the customers were all so hurried and so eager in the hopeful promise of the day, that they tumbled up against each other at the door, crashing their wicker baskets wildly, and left their purchases upon the counter, and came running back to fetch them, and committed hundreds of the like mistakes, in the best humour possible; while the Grocer and his people were so frank and fresh that the polished hearts with which they fastened their aprons behind might have been their own, worn outside for general inspection, and for Christmas daws to peck at if they chose.

But soon the steeples called good people all, to church and chapel, and away they came, flocking through the streets in their best clothes, and with their gayest faces. And at the same time there emerged from scores of bye-streets, lanes, and nameless turnings, innumerable people, carrying their dinners to the baker' shops. The sight of these poor revellers appeared to interest the Spirit very much, for he stood with Scrooge beside him in a baker's doorway, and taking off the covers as their bearers passed, sprinkled incense on their dinners from his torch. And it was a very uncommon kind of torch, for once or twice when there were angry words between some dinner-carriers who had jostled each other, he shed a few drops of water on them from it, and their good humour was restored directly. For they said, it was a shame to quarrel upon Christmas Day. And so it was. God love it, so it was.

From *A Christmas Carol*

CHARLES DICKENS was born on 7 February 1812 in Portsmouth. His father was a clerk in the Navy Pay Office who often ended up in financial trouble. When Dickens was twelve years old he moved to London and was sent to work in a shoe polish factory because his father had been imprisoned for debt. London made a permanent mark on the young Dickens – he loved it, drew inspiration from it, and it formed the basis of his strong social conscience. His career as a writer started in 1833 when his short stories and essays began to appear in newspapers and magazines. Many novels followed and Dickens became a celebrity in America and Britain. Charles Dickens died on 9 June 1870. He is buried in Westminster Abbey.

RECOMMENDED BOOKS BY CHARLES DICKENS:

Great Expectations
A Tale of Two Cities
Oliver Twist

GREAT EXPECTATIONS

Pip's life as an ordinary country boy is destined to be unexceptional until a chain of mysterious events lead him away from his humble origins and up the social ladder. His efforts to become a London gentleman bring him into contact not just with the upper classes but also with dangerous criminals. Pip's desire to improve himself is matched only by his longing for the icy-hearted Estella, but secrets from the past impede his progress and he has many hard lessons to learn.

'I would always prefer to go get another Dickens off the shelf than pick up a new book by someone I've not read yet . . . I love the tradition of Dickens, where even the most minor walk-on characters are twitching and particular and alive' Donna Tartt

'No story in the first person was ever better told' George Gissing

'As trim as a whippet. Touch any part of it and the whole structure quivers into life' Robert Douglas Fairhurst

'It is not the story of a boy who got too big for his boots, but of a child who, like all children, was perfectly entitled to begin life with great expectations' Alison Light

VINTAGE MINIS

The Vintage Minis bring you the world's greatest writers on the experiences that make us human. These stylish, entertaining little books explore the whole spectrum of life – from birth to death, and everything in between. Which means there's something here for everyone, whatever your story.

Desire	Haruki Murakami
Love	Jeanette Winterson
Marriage	Jane Austen
Babies	Anne Enright
Language	Xiaolu Guo
Motherhood	Helen Simpson
Fatherhood	Karl Ove Knausgaard
Family	Mark Haddon
Summer	Laurie Lee
Jealousy	Marcel Proust
Sisters	Louisa May Alcott
Home	Salman Rushdie
London	Charles Dickens
Race	Toni Morrison
Independence	Charlotte Brontë
Liberty	Virginia Woolf
Swimming	Roger Deakin
Friendship	Rose Tremain
Work	Joseph Heller
Money	Yuval Noah Harari
Austerity	Yanis Varoufakis
Injustice	Richard Wright

War	Sebastian Faulks
Murder	Arthur Conan Doyle
Depression	William Styron
Therapy	Stephen Grosz
Lies	Oscar Wilde
Drinking	John Cheever
Recovery	Helen Macdonald
Eating	Nigella Lawson
Parties	F. Scott Fitzgerald
Rave	Irvine Welsh
Psychedelics	Aldous Huxley
Art	Simon Schama
Calm	Tim Parks
Dreams	Sigmund Freud
Ghosts	M. R. James
Religion	Karen Armstrong
Science	Ian McEwan
Power	William Shakespeare
Freedom	Margaret Atwood
Death	Julian Barnes